Regret No More

SEB KIRBY
REGRET NO MORE

CANELO

First published in the United Kingdom in 2013 by Seb Kirby

This edition published in the United Kingdom in 2020 by

Canelo Digital Publishing Limited
Third Floor, 20 Mortimer Street
London W1T 3JW
United Kingdom

A CIP catalogue record for this book is available from the British Library.

Print ISBN 978 1 78863 934 7
Ebook ISBN 978 1 78863 654 4

Look for more great books at www.canelo.co

Printed and bound in Great Britain by Clays Ltd, Elcograf S.p.A.

*The secret of great fortunes without apparent cause
is a crime forgotten, for it was properly done.*

Honore de Balzac, *Le Pere Goriot* (1835)

Prologue

Alain Bellard had carried out few stranger jobs than this one.

The Fuseau Gallery in Hagedet in the Hautes-Pyrenees was well defended by conventional standards. It had the latest electronic security with state of the art laser beam scrutiny. This was quite useless since they had made a cardinal mistake. It would be no match for him.

In another life he'd been a consultant advising on the protection of valuable works of art and the essential advice he'd given all of his clients was this – do not depend on electronic security alone. He didn't do that kind of work any more. This paid much better. And no one had given that essential advice to the owners of the Fuseau Gallery.

They had been clever in concealing the sound sensors and invisible beams that kicked in when you disabled the main system. It might have fooled a lesser thief. But he was delayed only a few minutes while he dealt with the backup system.

The gallery was his. He could take whatever he wished.

This was what made this job such a strange one. He was to take just one painting – Picasso's 1937 portrait *Weeping Woman*.

How was it that Picasso painted so many pictures of this same woman, his lover Dora Maar, and all of them were so valuable? It didn't seem right. When the genius at the height of his powers could produce twenty, maybe even thirty, paintings like this in a month, how could each be worth millions?

It wasn't his concern.

He removed the painting from its hanging place and placed it on the floor. He wrapped it in the dark blue cotton sheet he'd brought with him, placed it under his arm and walked out of the gallery. To demonstrate his mastery, once outside, he reset the alarm system. The remaining paintings inside would be free from harm.

There was no overnight guard. If they were using CCTV cameras, they would learn little. His face was covered. The waiting vehicle was stolen and he would soon abandon it.

As he drove away down the steep mountainside road, he thought again about the instructions for the job.

He should take the painting and place it in one of the lockers in Oloron-Sainte-Marie railway station. He'd been given key number 109 for this purpose. Inside, he would find his payment for the night's work. Half a million euros. Half a lifetime working as a security consultant. It did not cross his mind to renege on the deal and fail to leave the painting. He knew better than to double cross those who had commissioned the theft.

Yes, it was a strange job. The more so since his final instruction was to wait six months and then tell the local police where the painting could be found.

Day 1

Present Day
Monday August 19th

Chapter 1

It was one of those calls, the kind you know are going to be menacing even before you pick up the phone.

I could have expected another cold call but I knew from the first that this was something more.

"Mr. Blake, we have an investment opportunity for you." It was an American voice, coming from one of those boiler rooms where you could hear the other operatives in the background placing similar calls.

I tried to keep calm. "There's no one named Blake here. You have the wrong number."

The caller continued. "I know you need the money, that you're in over your head. This one's a cert. Bestridge Investments. It's about to surge. I can show you the proof. You wouldn't be able to forgive yourself if you didn't make the most of this opportunity."

"I'm not interested. I'm not in over my head. You've called the wrong person."

"Don't get fooling with us, James. We know what your exposure is."

"I don't have any exposure. It's just a mistake. I'm ending this call."

I hit the end call key.

I turned to Julia. She couldn't hide her concern. "Trouble?"

The bump in her belly was so prominent now. It was just weeks to go before our son would be born. The ultrasound pictures showed the little man lying there at peace, waiting for his time to come shouting and screaming into the madness of this world.

"They've got our names. They say they're pushing investments, one of those boiler room scams, but I don't believe them. They know. The cover must be blown."

We were living as Charles and Mary Harrington. Three years had passed since the events in Florence that had nearly cost Julia her life. We'd moved from London to the Dorset countryside, just outside Weymouth. James and Julia Blake no longer existed. We'd built new lives. Julia was making a gradual but successful recovery.

The police promised no one would be able to find us once we were helped to change our identities. Nothing had come back in the last three years, not from Italy or from the Landos. But now there was this.

The Lando family operation had been slowed. Their illegal waste dumping scam was exposed for what it was. Alfieri and Matteo were dealt with. Alfieri was dead. Matteo was given a life sentence for his father's murder.

Yet Alessa Lando escaped punishment. Her lawyer, Santoni, created enough doubt in the mind of the jury that they were unable to be sure she'd been involved in the scam and the lawlessness that went with it. It was her husband, Alfieri, and her son, Matteo who were the real protagonists. She was acquitted.

We'd not been troubled. No one knew where to find us. Until now.

Neither of us wanted to say the Lando name out loud but we both knew that the day we'd feared throughout those three years was here.

I held Julia's hand. "Don't worry. I won't let any harm come to you or the baby."

Chapter 2

Wolfgang Heller shook his head – a gesture that would come close to costing two lives.

Here was this guy in the Jeep with the skinny blonde beside him and he was roaring down the street way too fast – here of all places, in this quiet suburb of San Diego in one of the pristine streets surrounding Mission Bay where respectable people raise kids, for God's sake. And, just as Heller was walking by and was about to cross the intersection with the neighbouring street, the guy in the Jeep insisted on cutting him up by turning into the side road at speed, causing Heller to make a sharp halt at the kerb as he passed.

That's what produced the shake of the head.

Now the driver had stopped the Jeep and was staring, as if his manhood was challenged in front of the blonde.

The head shook again.

The driver was coming out of the vehicle and starting to show rage.

"Hey fella, you got a problem? Shaking your head at me?"

He'd been working out, building up his muscles, Heller observed. He thought he was tough and he looked tough. OK, he would have frightened many a solid citizen with that pumped-up body and all that tattoo work. And,

8

of course, today Heller looked like a respectable, mild-mannered citizen, an easy touch. Why would he want to draw attention to himself in his line of work?

Heller shook his head again.

He let the driver come within touching distance, bringing him on with a smile. Before he could reach out, Heller struck. A double-fingered jab in both eyes all but blinded the oncomer. Unable to see, he was easy meat. Heller aimed a kick to the right leg and shattered the knee. The driver fell down, screaming. Heller stamped down hard on the nearest outstretched hand and heard the fingers crack. There was another scream. Then Heller shattered the other hand. The guy might never drive again.

Now, he had his boot on his neck. It would be easy to break the neck, to put this lesser mortal out of his misery forever. No, it was better to let him recover in agony. He aimed six punishing kicks to the groin. That would make servicing the blonde quite difficult for a few months to come. It was no surprise, then, that the driver passed out in this world of pain descending upon him.

The blonde was out of the vehicle, screaming at him, brandishing her mobile phone, yelling that she was calling the police. Heller walked straight over and kicked closed the door, trapping her hand. He heard her scream and, seeing the phone fall to the floor, he stamped the life out of it with his boot.

He threw the woman against the Jeep. He cuffed her hard across the face and held her beneath him. He could see the fear in her eyes, the heaving of those silicone breasts. He grabbed her nose and twisted it out of shape until she passed out. That would take more than a little plastic work to sort out.

Someone once told him only the truly psychotic could respond like this, without the need to go through the ritual of adrenalin arousal, the arguing, the shouting – like a coiled spring waiting to deploy at any time, in the moment, in the right here and now.

Was he psychotic? He did not think so. After all, he was the responsible citizen. People shouldn't drive with such disregard for others. Children would be playing in the streets if it wasn't for incompetents like this driving too fast and without due care.

He walked on. The police wouldn't be long in arriving. He would be gone by then. He wouldn't need to be in this town for long once the job was done.

Chapter 3

It was early evening. A vehicle was drawing up outside.

I looked through the window. It was too late to run now. Whoever it was out there, whoever it was coming for me and my family, we would now have to face them.

There was no outright attack. Just a polite ring of the doorbell.

He was American. A military-style buzz cut set off his determined, angular face. The eyes told of knowing determination. Yet the mouth was more appeasing.

"Jack Franks, FBI."

"There's nothing I can do for you. Please go."

"This won't take long. Let me inside and I'll let you know why I'm here."

I opened the door just wide enough for him to enter.

"So, Mr. Franks."

"Call me Jack."

"OK, Jack. Why are you here?"

"The boiler room call, we're sorry about that. We just had to know it was you."

"Just tell me why you're here."

"Voice recognition. We have voice patterns from the interviews you had with Inspector Manieri in Florence. We had to be sure you were here, James."

I tried to keep down my anger. "Look, I don't know what brings you here, but we just want to be left alone. My wife, can't you see she's expecting? Third trimester. We have a life to live."

Julia said nothing. Her blank stare was enough.

Franks nodded. "I understand."

"Show me some ID."

He pulled out his badge. "I'm out of Washington, not Langley."

"Didn't know you did international operations."

"Well, we do."

"Give us a reason why we should talk to you?"

He pulled out an iPad from the leather file case he was carrying. "Let me show you this."

He handed over the tablet with a video playing. The legend said: Sollicciano Prison (Florence). The video showed a face I knew and, though changed in the three years since I'd last seen it, one I recognised as Matteo Lando.

He was staring straight at the camera. Life in one of the toughest prisons in Europe hadn't been kind to him. His Latin good looks were fading fast. He had emptiness in his eyes that told of what it took to survive in such a place.

Franks knew he had me. "There's sound. Turn it up."

"How did you get this?"

"It's a Skype call. He thinks it's secure but we found a way of hacking it."

I turned up the sound. It wasn't clear who Matteo was talking to since there was no image of the replier. Yet this wasn't the most important thing on my mind, it was what Matteo was saying.

"A time will come when I can get out of here. My men will find a way. Meantime, I can do most of what I want to do from in here."

A man's voice. "But you want my help?"

"A debt I want to call in."

"Anything. You know I'd do anything you need."

"Blake. And his wife. The ones that got Emelia killed and put me in here. I want them. I want them killed."

"Why now? After all this time?"

"Because this could not come any sooner. And because they remain a threat to the family."

"They may not be easy to find. They will have new identities by now."

"To make it easier. A million dollars. A million dollars for each of them."

I turned back to Franks. "Tell me what I can do to help."

Chapter 4

Heller found the house he was looking for. Facing onto Mission Bay, it was just the type of place he would have liked for himself.

The whole area was pleasing. The Bay, artificially produced by excavating the bed of a local river, was a calm and reassuring sight. Joggers ran on the path circling the lake. Women on skateboards pushed toddlers in big-wheeled buggies. Young people exercised in that peculiar American power-walking way. Cyclists wheeled past. Heller knew he was with dependable, respectable people.

Across the narrow strip of land carrying Mission Bay Boulevard stood the Pacific Ocean with its bold, unpredictable waves crashing ashore. He thought now of how he'd sat in the waterfront bar the evening before looking out across the ocean as the huge sun had dipped below the horizon and he'd wondered at a view that took the eye all the way to Japan. And, yes, in the twilight, he had seen the green flash.

It was a designer house, built in the last five years in faux Art Deco style. A large central stairwell ran all the way up through the house to a flat-topped roof where you could sunbathe in privacy. Rooms led off the central stairwell. They were not stuffy square enclosures. They retained a circular, open symmetry and were more like spaces to be used for studying or relaxing or sleeping. It was a pleasing and challenging construct.

It was easy to break in and look around. There was no one here. The targets must have been tipped off. That was worrying. It meant the assignment would take more time and more ingenuity than expected.

He knew from his search of the house that they would not be back. Such knowledge came with experience of having done this many times before. Those small personal things were missing, the kind of things you would take if you left in a hurry. The family laptops, the wife's jewellery and cosmetics, the photos of the kids, were all missing. There was no point waiting for them to return or searching further. The family had been moved.

It was time to leave. Time to reassess.

Chapter 5

Agent Franks had my full attention.

"So, James, you can see why we had to get to you as a matter of urgency. To warn you. You, your wife and child."

I didn't like the way he said "child". The thought that he might have known about Julia's pregnancy before he made contact, that he'd somehow factored this into his pitch, made the hairs on the back of my neck stand up.

I looked shaken, I know. "If you can find us, the Landos can find us. And that's before they place two million dollars on the table. But why are you helping us?"

He leaned closer. "I have to tell you I wouldn't be here if there weren't national security issues involved. This is not only about Matteo Lando and his threat to you."

Julia interrupted. "It's about Alessa Lando, isn't it?"

Franks turned to her. "We know she left Italy after her acquittal. We traced her to South America but then she disappeared."

That did nothing to calm my fears. "So, do we know who Matteo was talking to in the Skype call?"

Franks sought to be reassuring but his words had the opposite effect. "No. We traced the call but the trail was dead by the time we could get there to check it out. It was made from a bar somewhere in Tijuana but the bar owner couldn't or wouldn't recall anything."

"So what do you want?"

"We want to protect you."

"In return for what?"

"In return for your help in finding Alessa Lando."

"And what makes you think I would be of any help? You must have so many more able people?"

"We know what you did in Florence, James. How you got under the Lando's skin. How you blew them apart. We think if anyone can find a way to Alessa Lando it's you."

"You mean you want to use us as bait."

"I didn't say that."

I could feel my anger rising. "Then what would it be if it wasn't that? Now Matteo's coming after my family, you think you can find a way to use that to ensnare him and then somehow smoke out Alessa."

Franks glanced over at Julia again. "You have a lot to lose, James. We're dealing with people who will stop at nothing to avenge what they see as a wrong against them."

"So, this is a threat, isn't it? You'll lead Matteo to us if that's the only way of getting to Alessa?"

"I'm not saying that. Just that if there were others on my side who might be thinking along those lines we could talk them out of it if you offered a better way to get to her."

"And it's just a coincidence that Matteo has waited all this time to come after us?"

He didn't answer. "Look, I'm here to help. Accept that help."

17

With that, he stood to take his leave. "Think about it, James. What's best for you and your family. We'll talk again in the morning."

Julia came and sat close as we waited for the sound of Franks' vehicle to fade into the distance. "Jim. Tell me it hasn't started all over again."

I couldn't get Agent Franks' words from my mind.

You have a lot to lose, James.

It was a threat. And what he'd said was right.

In the three years since Julia's escape from Florence, we'd built a new life as the Harringtons. No one would have called it glamorous but we had most of what we wanted and we were happy.

I had a job in Weymouth, giving mortgage advice with The Dorset Building Society. It wasn't as interesting as my work in London with the radio station but it had its merits. Helping young couples find a way to move into their own home for the first time was a reason for quiet satisfaction.

Julia had found work in a gift shop that sold paintings and pottery produced by local artists. It was a long way from her career in conservation at the Clinton Ridley Studio in Mayfair but, again, her work had its interests and satisfactions as she saw local artists making sales of their work.

The Dorset Building Society encouraged employees to work with local charities and I was now a volunteer with the Weymouth Food Bank on The Esplanade. Local families came to collect food twice a month.

What the families needed was work and money. What they got, with the recession biting deep in places like Weymouth, was help to put just enough food on the table to keep their family together. It was a blow to the self-esteem of each and every one of them to come to the Food Bank and ask for help; I knew that. I felt the anger and shame of every one of them. My troubled upbringing in Birmingham had left me with no illusions about what they were going through.

It wasn't all about hardship. I was coaching football again and had risen to the rank of deputy manager of a team of fifteen year-olds who played in the Weymouth League on Sundays. They were as committed and as enthusiastic as the players I'd coached in London. The lads played each match to win and tried hard to apply the tactics I was teaching them.

It wasn't glamorous but it was what we wanted.

Julia was recovering from the ordeal of Florence. It would take more time but she was gaining perspective every day on what had happened.

She'd taken a break from work to prepare for the birth of our baby. The prospect of our first child was the greatest satisfaction of all.

We were safe.

We were happy.

We did not want anything to change.

Chapter 6

It was a short drive yet it was a million miles away if you were on the wrong side.

The responsibilities of Wolfgang Heller's profession demanded high-class travel but with anonymity, so he was making the drive across the border to Mexico in a hired Buick. It was big enough to be comfortable yet not ostentatious enough to get him noticed.

The border crossing looked like any other tollbooth at an expressway where you pulled up and paid the fee. That was until you noticed the lines of vehicles held up on the opposite lanes trying to get in being hauled over to be searched. You could enter the Third World with ease but leaving it was another matter. Heller was waved through into Mexico with a nod and no need to show his passport.

The assembly plants nestling just on the Mexico side soon gave way to the desert and the giant fence that kept the world out from the US. Here and there he could make out the crude wooden crosses left on the high wire mesh fence to commemorate those who had tried to make it into the land of prosperity but had failed. There was a large number of them. For Heller there was no excuse for failure no matter what the circumstances. He shouted as he drove past. "Losers!"

It was just a short hop to Tijuana and Avenue de la Revolucion, a flea-bitten strip with gift shops selling knock-off watches, with poisonous cafes and countless stores selling cloned prescription drugs to an American middle class that couldn't afford them in their own country. And off the main strip, there were the prostitute dens and the all-day joints dealing in drugs. No wonder the whole town was so poor when everyone was trying to sell the same things. No wonder that the whole place was presided over by a painted donkey passed off as a zebra. And no wonder that there were twelve other painted donkeys lying in wait. The paucity of the illusion reminded him of everything he found unsatisfactory about the town.

Yet the Landos had a history here. Heller would never have come to a town like this but he knew if he worked for Matteo he would have to tolerate the place as long as he wanted it that way.

Heller would have to find a way of telling him that the hit had not succeeded, that the target in San Diego was no longer there when he called.

Chapter 7

It was approaching eight PM when two police vehicles drew up outside the house. I could see three silhouetted figures through the glass in the front door. One of them reached out and rang the doorbell.

"Charles Harrington?"

"Yes."

I opened the door a crack.

"Can we come in? We have some questions."

He was young and he introduced himself as Detective Inspector Martin Reid. His two uniformed colleagues stood silent beside him.

"Can't we do this some other time? My wife is sleeping."

"That would be Mary Harrington?"

"Yes. Who else?"

"It's urgent. We'll take up as little of your time as necessary."

I opened the door to let them in.

"How do you know Agent Franks?"

His eyes were taking in the disorder in the room. It looked bad, I know. We'd decided we couldn't stay here after Franks' visit. Julia went to bed to rest but couldn't sleep. I started packing everything we might need into our travel luggage. Now it was sitting there as suspicious as a murder of crows, evidence waiting to be collected.

I decided to stall. "Agent Franks?"

He showed me a photograph of Franks that looked like it had been taken from a records database. "Do you know him? It's a simple enough question."

The two million dollar price on our heads meant we could trust no one. Money of that order loosened tongues. That applied even to those as dependable looking as DI Reid.

"I don't know him. Why are you asking me this?"

He told me Franks had been found dead. Franks had used his satellite navigation to find us on his visit here and our coordinates were still programmed into the machine. The police knew exactly where to come.

I wanted to ask how Franks had died but I knew any concern I showed would be interpreted as proof I was lying. I had to show no interest.

"I'm sorry for his loved ones, Inspector, but I have to tell you this means nothing to me."

"Even though we found the co-ordinates to this house on his satellite navigation?"

"I can't be held responsible for that. Maybe he had a reason to come here."

"And what might that be?"

"How could I know? He never came. I've never met him. He could even have had the wrong address."

"So you can't help."

"How could I?"

DI Reid's attention returned to the luggage. "You're thinking of traveling?"

"Annual holiday. We're visiting my mother in Edinburgh."

"I think you'll understand that we'll need to keep in close touch with you. In case we have further questions."

"Of course." I gave him a false address in Edinburgh. "You can contact us there."

Within an hour of their leaving I had the luggage packed into the Land Rover and Julia and I were on our way to London.

It would not take Reid long to realise I'd given him a false address which in itself would tell him I wasn't being straight with him. But this was preferable to waiting it out in the house not knowing who would get to know we were there.

Chapter 8

Alvaro Gutierrez liked the fear that came to all around him when anyone spoke his adopted name, El Romero.

As El Romero he had a reputation. The trademark enforcement of his will was to return the bodies of those who had gone against him to their families with their hands cut off and their tongues ripped out.

His power extended to every aspect of life in the Baja. Those in the police and in local government who were not on his payroll were so aware of the dangers of taking on his Soto cartel that they offered no threat. Some said he was the most important man in Baja, if not in the whole of Mexico.

To be feared and to be hated were necessary evils to maintain the absolute control over the Soto cartel that was required if he and each and every one of its members were to survive. The pickings were rich indeed, fuelled by those well-dressed and well-educated gringos who couldn't get enough of the cocaine he shipped up from Columbia.

Absolute loyalty, absolute control was essential if they were to defeat the twin evils that stalked them. The Vargas cartel headed by Johnny Rivenza was a constant menace, all the time trying to move in on the Baja when it had been agreed amongst the council of cartel owners in the whole of Mexico that the territory belonged to El Romero. And there was Pedro Martinez, the new chief of police who, like so many before him, had threatened to close down the cartels and the drugs trade with them. Unlike the others, Martinez had not been swayed by the promise of money or threats to himself and his family. There were even those who were saying Martinez was in this for real.

So, sad to say, the conflict around El Romero had cost lives. He wished it didn't have to be that way but this was about survival, pure and simple.

He turned to Luiz Reyas, his right hand man, who was waiting for his instructions. When recruited Reyas had twenty small star tattoos on his right forearm, meaning he'd killed twenty men. Now the number was over one hundred. It was a testament to the difficult times in which they lived.

"Luiz, I want you to keep a close watch on the German."

"Senor Heller?"

El Romero nodded. "I don't trust him. I want to know everything he does."

Luiz replied, "You have my best efforts, El Romero. But it will not be easy to keep track of such a man."

"Luiz, I can help. Rui will place a tracker in the German's phone."

El Romero had confidence in Rui Velasquez who was to the cartel all things technical. He had the skills needed to keep surveillance on police and military radio and Internet communications. He provided the means they drew on to find safe passage across the border with the consignments and he was expert at bugging rooms and phones. The lives of Soto members too many to count had been saved by his intelligence.

Luiz wasn't yet convinced. "There will be problems if Heller finds out."

"He will not. Velasquez has never failed to find a way. He'll steal the phone while Heller sleeps, fit the bug and replace it. The German will never know."

El Romero's thoughts turned to how he'd become involved with the German. It had been difficult to agree to help. El Romero had thought long and hard before saying yes. But he did owe an obligation to Alfieri Lando who all those years ago had sent men to the Baja to help him seize control and establish the cocaine route into the US and, as a reward for Alfieri's help, into Italy. With Alfieri dead, what else could he do when Matteo came to him to ask for the favour of assisting Heller in his mission in the United States? There were problems enough here in Tijuana, he knew all too well, without bringing in new, difficult to understand problems from outside. Yet an obligation is what it was and he'd agreed.

It was different with the earlier obligation, the matter of the Blakes. Matteo had spoken as if he should know them, a sign, perhaps of his isolation when seeing events pass before him from prison. There were those in Europe who were better placed than him to capture the two million. Life was complicated enough here. He was content that he'd discharged the obligation by contacting the right people there.

Luiz broke the train of thought. "The German is back."

El Romero looked up as Wolfgang Heller was shown into the room. "Well?"

Heller kept eye contact, even though his body posture told that he had not brought positive news. "The house in

San Diego was empty. The Ravitz family was no longer there."

"A tip off?"

"Is there another way of explaining it?"

Why did the German make everything he said into an accusation?

El Romero tried not to show his pleasure at the thought of Heller leaving again sooner than planned. "A message from Matteo. You're needed in Austin."

Heller looked straight back. "I'll be out of here on the first plane."

Chapter 9

The late night traffic was light as I steered our Land Rover onto the motorway that would take us to London.

It hadn't taken long to get going. We'd decided to shed our identities as Mary and Charles Harrington. We would soon be found if we continued to use anything in their names and going back to Julia and James Blake was also out of the question. So, cash and new identities would be required, at least until we could find a way past the threat to our family.

It had felt like I was staging a robbery as I'd used the Harrington bank card for the last time in the ATM in the deserted street in Weymouth before we'd set out. The cash appeared in the form of fifty crisp twenty pound notes. When I'd tried to repeat the request, the machine displayed a polite 'refer to your bank' message and offered no more money.

There was no doubt this would add to police suspicion but there was no other choice.

As we travelled on there was an intense shower of rain that lowered visibility and meant I had to concentrate fully on the road ahead. Julia, sitting beside me in the front seat, had concerns that would not wait. "Are you sure we should be doing this, Jim?"

She'd fought back well from what happened in Florence. It had been three years of steady recovery from the trauma of the sexual degradation that Alfieri Lando had subjected her to and three years of steady recovery from the heroin addiction he'd forced upon her. Her recovery was based on establishing routine around known events at known times that could hold no threat. The news that we were expecting our first child after so many years of hoping had given her a real lift. Preparing for the birth of our son had become an important part of the healing routine.

I knew what was troubling her. "The antenatal appointments."

"We're going to miss them."

"We can get into the antenatal system in London. I'm sure it's every bit as good."

"I wish we didn't have to run like this with so little time to prepare."

I tried to calm her. "The important thing is you leave the worrying to me. We can find a way through this."

She managed a smile. She looked as beautiful as ever.

I told her that the danger we'd been placed in posed the greater risk, not just to us but to our child.

"What choice do we have? Our cover is blown. The threat from Matteo Lando is immediate, I'm sure of it. And if the FBI can find us, the Landos or anyone else after the reward will be able to find us if we stay where we are."

"I know that, Jim. But I wish there was another way. The FBI. Maybe they would help?"

"We'll try to get their help. And help from the police. But only when we're somewhere no one will be able to find us."

As I drove on, Julia checked for news on her iPad. "It's here. A local news report from the Weymouth newspaper."

Man found dead in abandoned vehicle appears to have been shot. Police await post mortem result.

"And no mention of the FBI?"

She stroked the screen to make sure she had the full story. "It could be just that the reporter hasn't been able to file the whole story yet."

"Or, the FBI doesn't want it to be known they're involved."

"Jim, why would they want to do that?"

"It happens."

"You're making me more scared."

"I didn't mean it to come out that way."

"So we run."

"We run. And then we find out who we can trust."

We travelled on until the traffic slowed as we came off the motorway near Hounslow and began to pass through the London suburbs.

Eight million people. A good place to hide.

I know now I should have paid more attention to the black SUV that had been behind us since we'd set out. Thinking back, it wasn't difficult to see that it was following at just the optimum distance to maintain contact but not be seen. I was more concerned with Julia and with the safety of our son to notice if it was a tail and too concerned with all the questions about the nature of the threat against us.

Chapter 10

No one would choose to come to Texas in midsummer but this was the place selected by the one who would tell him where the targets had fled. Wolfgang Heller cursed this lack of sense.

At 103 degrees downtown Austin was a desolate place. Perhaps it was the heat that led Heller to imagine he could still smell the stale stench of slavery but he chose not to dwell on this. He could be anonymous here, check into the *Gambit Hotel* just off 6th Street and spend the night in the blues bars clustered in the half-dozen run down blocks in what passed for night-life in this town.

He knew he would not find the family in this downtown area. They would be accommodated in some better place, somewhere clean and light with fresher air, some place where those of wealth lived in ignorance of what happened here. He would have to find the targets in that safer world but this was for the coming days and tonight he was going to enjoy himself.

He found her in the *Crazy Diamond* looking for all the world like one of the strippers on a night off. But she told him she worked in the cafe just down the hill from the Capitol building and that she'd stayed in town because she wanted some action.

They talked, shouted in fact, against the high volume of the jump band. She made no comment about his German accent and asked no questions about why he was here in Austin. Within an hour she was back in his hotel room taking off her clothes for him.

Heller hated to see the tattoos as she undressed. He did not think a woman should mutilate her body like that. It made him want to hurt her and as they made love he tried his hardest to do just that, to punish her for her vanity. But the more he tried to hurt her, the more pleasure she took from him. He didn't want to kill her. She didn't deserve it. He wanted more than that from her. He wanted to drain her sensuality to enhance his power, to recharge the tantric energy that gave him control over the world. She obeyed without complaint, though he was sure she knew she had no choice. After two hours on the bed together, he came to a sudden stop and asked her to dress and leave.

She knew enough to not complain and soon he was alone on the bed, listening to the loud, low rumbling of the hundred or so air conditioning units in place on the back wall of the hotel, a guarantee that no one would sleep this night.

He lay there thinking of how, the next day, he would make the hit. Make it swift and sweet.

Chapter 11

Alessa Lando had found happiness where she'd least expected to find it.

The dark days with Alfieri were over. Now, she'd begun a new life.

Dmitri Kolokov was everything she'd ever wanted in a man. He was powerful and ruthless. His companies controlled the minerals trade not just in much of Russia but also throughout half of Africa. He'd survived the Soviet system and come out of it as an oligarch, one of the fifty richest men in the world. Yes, he'd known trauma in this life yet he was calm and collected and knew nothing of the torment of a man like Alfieri.

She couldn't believe love had returned so late in her life. But love is what it was, passionate and unstinted. She and Dmitri were like first time youngsters. Why, when he could have any woman he wanted did he want her to be so much a part of his life? Perhaps he needed the attentions of a powerful woman like herself. Perhaps it was a miracle best left to be what it was, for itself, without further need for thought.

She liked his courtesy and kindness when he was with her. But most of all she liked his power. It was the love of power that bound them together. It energised them both. It was the great aphrodisiac.

Yet now this security she'd found was threatened by something from her past that was long supposed to be forgotten. They were out there. People determined to find her and kill her.

She had responded. With Matteo's help, she'd taken the initiative. She was determined to run them down before they could find her. That train of events was now underway. With the Kolokov power to shield her, she would prevail.

But there was a nagging doubt that refused to go away no matter how much she tried to tell herself that concern over this small matter wasn't needed. She couldn't be sure the Blakes were not involved in these latest threats. She couldn't forgive herself for how she'd underestimated them in the events in Florence that brought her family so low. And, unable to shake off those doubts, she'd taken the required steps.

It was surprising how long it had taken her dear Matteo to exert his authority in Sollicciano. Now he'd reached the top there, life would be better for him. She was pleased she'd been able to call on his help in the matter of the Blakes, as with much else that was a threat to her.

Alessa looked over at Dmitri as he lay sleeping in the bed beside her. Yes, it would all be right.

She'd changed her name long before she met Dmitri and changed it again when she'd become the third Mrs. Kolokov – not that any of the Russians ever called her that.

In his line of business, he required twenty-four-hour security protection. Three men guarded the house around the clock.

No one knew she was here. Even if her location was discovered, she was protected.

She would be safe with Dmitri here in London.

Yet the report she'd received from Mexico telling her that the hit on the Ravitz family in San Diego had been unsuccessful was worrying. All the more reason to make sure there were no loose ends.

Chapter 12

The Allegro Hotel in a run-down part of Bloomsbury looked like the no-questions-asked place we needed, but getting them to accept us as we were wasn't going to be easy.

"You have no ID?" The receptionist, a young Pole, spoke good English. She had a practiced efficiency that told you all you needed to know about why she had a job while half a million locals were without work.

The excuse I used had been rehearsed a hundred times on the drive into London. "I made the mistake of placing all my cards and other ID in a new leather wallet. I was so pleased the way it organised everything. And then it was stolen. I'm sure it was someone who brushed past me at the train station but by the time I realised it was gone, it was too late."

She wasn't convinced. "And your wife? She has no ID, either?"

"She forgot her purse. Left it at home when we set out."

"So, you have nothing to identify yourselves. How do you propose to pay the bill?"

"I have cash."

This made her more suspicious. "I have to refer it to the manager."

There was the sound of their talking for a long time behind a screen as the receptionist made her concerns known. The manager appeared at the reception desk and looked us over. "You have a vehicle?"

I lied. "We arrived by train." I didn't want to give him the registration number. We could have been easily traced from that. I'd left the Land Rover nearby and we'd walked in. It was no use to us. The vehicle itself could be traced. We'd arrived with just one of the suitcases, more to show we had the kind of possessions that normal visitors would. My plan was that if we could get a room at the hotel I could bring the rest of the luggage in and then leave the vehicle somewhere it would be stolen.

The manager eyed the suitcase and then both of us. "You know this is something I shouldn't be doing." His gaze dwelt on Julia's bump. "But, bearing in mind your wife's condition and the lateness of the hour, I'll allow it. But, I expect you to provide identification details within forty-eight hours. Understood?"

I agreed and thanked him. We signed in as John and Elizabeth Meredith.

Room 316 was at the rear of the hotel. It lacked space but was otherwise acceptable.

I lay beside Julia on the bed. "We've made it."

She managed a smile. "I wish it felt better than it does."

I showed her both our phones with the batteries removed. The iPad had been closed down long before we reached London. "No one knows we're here. For a while at least. We should find a way to contact Miles."

Julia frowned.

I knew there was no point in pretending otherwise. The relationship between Julia and my brother, Miles, was damaged almost beyond repair. Would she ever be able to forgive him for placing her in the hands of the Landos when he suggested she should contact them to access their art collection in her search for a masterpiece?

For his part, Miles couldn't forgive himself for ever having thought this was a proper thing to have done, knowing, as he did, that the corruption in the Lando family was certain to place her in danger. It was a misjudgement he would have to live with for the rest of his life. The suggestion that he was so driven to break the story of the Lando's illegal waste dumping activity, that he became oblivious to the danger he'd placed her in, was what kept him awake at night. What Julia was subjected to at the hands of Alfieri Lando was something he hadn't come to terms with.

Julia, in her turn, wanted nothing to do with Miles. It was her way of closing her mind to what had happened.

Her voice was weak. "Do we have to see him?"

"He's in London. And we need help."

I bought an access card from reception and used the hotel guest computer. I requested a new email account in a false name. Confirmation came back by return. I used the new account to send a message to Miles.

Need your help, bro. Pls reply to this address.

He would know what it meant.

Day 2

Tuesday August 20th

Chapter 13

Julia wished she could just stay still for the next three weeks. She trusted Jim's judgment and she could see why they needed to be running like this. Yet it didn't feel right.

When she felt her baby kick, as he was kicking now, her world had only this one centre, this one purpose – to bring this new life into the world.

She knew the time would come, in the hours and days before the birth, when she would have energy without limit. Then she would be ready for the great day to come. But right now she wanted safety and security and the absence of worry, for the benefit of herself and their son. And all the energy had drained from her body.

It wasn't like her to be passive like this. She'd not been afraid to live her own life and fight with the best of them to be a success. That was where Jim was such a good partner in her life. He'd never tried to stand in the way of her wish to achieve in her own right. Before Florence, before the Landos, her ambition was to make her name as the most famous of art restorers. That ambition remained, though she was less sure than ever how this might now be achieved.

She was alarmed that James was turning to his brother Miles for help. She'd tried everything to forgive Miles for bringing the Landos into her life but she still couldn't find a place for him in her heart. It wasn't just what had happened to her and the way she'd been delivered into the hands of Alfieri Lando. It was what had happened to her sister, Emelia.

It was the cruellest of fates that she'd found her sister after all those years, only to lose her within a few days. Without Miles, she would never have known of Emelia's existence. It would have been best if she'd never gone to Florence and tried to help her sister escape. Emelia might be alive today and that was a torture Julia couldn't find her way past.

She blamed Miles for that. And for giving her those few days of false hope and for making her complicit in Emelia's death.

Julia tried to imagine being in the same room again with Miles and not wanting to begin hitting him and not stop.

Now James was planning to meet Miles. The prospect of that filled her with dread.

She was sure of one thing – the need to eat.

The restaurant downstairs was basic. It would have to do. James would be hungry too.

Chapter 14

Miles Blake stared at the email message he'd just picked up on his phone. He hoped it was spam but he knew in his heart it couldn't be brushed aside. His brother was in trouble.

He tapped in the reply.

Where are you?

He knew he'd have to wait for the response. James would be using some form of public Internet access and would only be able to check back once in a while.

His mind turned to thoughts of Julia, the trauma she'd been through at the hands of the Landos and how he was still finding it difficult to absolve himself of the guilt of what he'd done. Now these thoughts turned to the loss of Sergio, his photographer, colleague and friend. His determination to break the Lando story was seen by some to have led to Sergio's death. Such thoughts about Julia and about Sergio fuelled the contents of the dark dreams that came each night.

Yet he'd not given up on the goal of righting the wrongs. The hope of achieving that rested with finishing what he'd started. He was using his investigative skills to achieve what the Italian justice system could not – to bring down Alessa Lando.

He'd discussed this with James over a year ago but he'd been dismissive.

"If the Italian prosecutor couldn't succeed in implicating Alessa, what makes you think you could do better?"

Miles had been sure of himself. "Because there's another way. When the Landos got control of the drugs business in Northern Italy, they seemed to come from nowhere. One day they were also-rans, the next they were kingpins. Rumour was they had a secret supply route direct from South America. You know me and secrets?"

"You don't believe in them?"

"I've never believed in them. Every secret is a point of weakness and an opportunity. If only you're determined enough to prize it open."

"And you think you have a lead?"

Miles had smiled. "Those rumours had it that Alessa Lando was involved from the start in the Landos gaining supremacy. That she was the catalyst."

James had not been convinced. "It was a long time ago. I don't see where you're coming from."

And they'd left it at that.

Miles realised now that when they met he would have to tell his brother just how far he'd got with this line of investigation and tell Julia, if she would listen to him.

The email client pinged. Miles checked the messages.

There was a reply from James.

Meet at Charing Cross in an hour.

Chapter 15

Next morning Wolfgang Heller showered and took breakfast in the hotel lounge. The waitress, a young blonde, disliked him from the start. When she heard him talking in English with a young academic from Oxford who was visiting Texas University, matters got worse.

Heller was saying that no one in this town knew the meaning of politeness and the academic agreed. They'd both had similar experiences since arriving in town. The academic told him how he'd visited the art gallery where they had a display by a local artist who textured and treated old books and assembled them as sculpture. When he'd tried to ask about the artist and if he was well-known outside Austin, the gallery attendant had treated him with scorn, despising his Englishness and his interest in art. The academic was left wondering what the attendant was doing working in the gallery when she despised modern art and felt the right to be unpleasant to those that came to admire it.

Heller confided that he'd had a similar experience. When he'd come to the reception desk to complain about the noise of the air conditioning and to ask for a transfer to another room, he'd been told the hotel was full and he would not be allowed to change. But that wasn't the

47

real problem. It was the lack of politeness with which the hotel manager had treated the request that bothered him.

The young blonde heard all this but showed no apparent concern as she took the breakfast orders of the two men. She was gone in the kitchen for longer than might be expected. Looking back on what occurred, Heller should have taken that as a sign. Nor could he be sure that when she returned there wasn't an amused expression on her face.

Some minutes later a fat chef emerged from the kitchen. He was morbidly obese, the kind of condition that could only have arisen if he ate as much of the food in the kitchen he could before the hotel proprietor noticed the impact on the food bill. The fat chef stood near the doorway of his kitchen and looked at them for a long time. Again, looking back, Heller knew this should have alerted him to what was to come.

They cooked him an omelette. The waitress placed it before him with a smile and a cheery comment. He cut into it and took in the first mouthful. It was hot and well cooked with just enough of the egg at its centre left runny, just the way a good omelette should be. He looked down at the plate to load his second mouthful and noticed something white and liquid oozing from the centre. He opened it with his fork. There it was – phlegm and spittle, and from more than one of them. As a mark of their true hospitality, these citizens of Austin had spat in his food and were even now from the safety of the kitchen laughing at what they'd done.

He said nothing. He placed his napkin on the table and lined up his knife and fork back on the plate.

The waitress returned. She was trying not to smile. She was mocking what he'd said by showing him just how polite she could be. "You're not finishing. We're so sorry you haven't enjoyed your meal. Is there anything else I can get you?"

Heller did not respond. "I'm not so hungry after all."

He said farewell to the academic and wished him well for his visit. He then went to his room and induced vomiting by placing his fingers down the back of his throat.

He was beyond anger. It was an unspeakable assault on his whole being. He had no idea what state of health the fat chef and the young blonde waitress enjoyed but he now had to share that with them. The fat chef did not look well. He could be a carrier for any one of a dozen debilitating diseases.

Heller waited. He sat in the lobby and watched as they cleared the breakfast area and the staff prepared to leave the hotel at the end of their early morning shift. He followed the fat chef out into the heat of the day, through the pre-noon haze to the apartment where the chef lived. He gave him a few minutes before entering the building, observing from the street the telltale movement of the window blinds on the second floor as the chef made himself at home.

It wasn't difficult to gain entry. The main entrance door was left open to allow circulation of whatever air was available on this hottest of days. Inside, he removed the folded white protective suit he'd carried in his pocket and pulled it on. He pulled on elasticated shoe covers, a hair cover and thin polymer gloves. He would leave no DNA trace. On the second floor, the chef's door was also unlocked. Heller was in and on him before he had time to cry for help. He forced open the mouth and yanked out the tongue. "This your idea of being polite?"

Heller released the tongue and waited for a reply.

The fat chef began to cry. Real tears. "Please, sir. I know it was wrong. But please don't do this."

Wolfgang had the hunting knife out. He frog-marched the fat chef to the shower. He slit the fat chef's nose, cut off his ears and forced them into his mouth. It was his way of saying that the mistake they had made wasn't just being impolite but it was the crime of not respecting the privacy of his breakfast conversation. It was a pathetic, bloody sight. The chef's eyes pleading to be let go. His blood staining his white chef's outfit and spattering Heller's protective suit.

He cut off the chef's clothing to leave him naked before him. As was always the case when faced with such sudden and arbitrary violence the chef was now mute. No need to be concerned any longer about his alerting anyone. Heller made one more cut with the knife, a long deep gash beneath the chef's sagging breasts and the man passed out. Heller began filleting him as if he were a side of meat, cutting deep into the bulbous flesh.

It was best to finish it. He'd made his point, after all. Heller thrust the knife into the chef's heart and then withdrew it. The chef jerked back to life and began convulsing. In five minutes he would be dead. There was justice in this world.

Another citizen, maybe many more, had been protected from the antisocial behaviour of men like this.

It made Wolfgang feel good, as any responsible person would.

It was time to clean up. He turned on the shower and watched the water turn red as it played over the dead chef's body. He severed the arms and legs with the hunting knife and then cut off the head.

In fifteen minutes the water stopped turning red. By then, Heller had pulled back the faded carpet in the adjoining room and had prised up the floorboards. Yes, there was enough space between this floor and the floor beneath to contain a dismembered body. He lined the space with rubbish sacks he took from the chef's tiny kitchen and transferred the body parts from the shower one by one before replacing the floorboards and the carpet. Heller was pleased with this and allowed himself a smile. In all probability, the body would not be discovered for weeks.

He had work to do this day and, in any case, he couldn't have followed them both. Soon enough, he would follow the young blonde waitress home and deal with her impoliteness.

Downstairs, he removed the blood-spattered protective suit, the hat and the shoes and placed them, together with the knife, in another of the plastic sacks he'd removed from the chef's kitchen. He walked five blocks and disposed of it in one of the waste bins in an alley close to nearby restaurants.

–

Luiz Reyas had followed the German to Austin. The tracker that Velasquez used to bug Heller's phone was working well.

Reyas watched as the German left the apartment and walked away along the street. He wondered why Senor Heller had spent so much time in that downtown apartment but knew better than to approach it too soon.

Chapter 16

Miles waited at Charing Cross station for two hours.

He made sure he covered all the possibilities. He checked both the Villiers Street and Strand entrances and checked each every twenty minutes in case James was coming in from the street. He checked the arrivals area in case he was coming in by train. Miles now sat in the coffee place near the Strand exit and tried to work out what had gone wrong.

He checked James' message again. It was clear. *Meet at Charing Cross in an hour.* Miles had arrived in half an hour and two hours had now elapsed. Something had detained James.

Miles tried to convince himself there was a mundane solution. James had never intended the email to be taken literally. Then why had he sent it? The message was meant for someone else and for another day and it had somehow appeared in his inbox. But James had no other brother. Something routine had happened that meant he couldn't keep the appointment. Then, why had he not sent another message? No, it was inescapable. James was in trouble and whatever it was had caught up with him before he could make his way to Charing Cross.

He needed to find from where James had sent the message. Knowing that Julia was nearing full term, it was a certainty they had been together when the message was sent. The location was unlikely to be Weymouth. James would not have been able to make it to the station in an hour from there. They must be on the move. That, in itself, was further fuel to the idea that they were in trouble. Julia would have wanted to limit any trips to an absolute minimum at this time.

It might be possible to find their location from the email. The email address in itself would not help. It was one of those anonymous handles that James must have adopted to save using his normal address in case it was being monitored. Yet there was a chance the location the message was sent from could be discovered from the encoding in the message and he knew someone who might be able to help.

It was one of the advantages of working as an investigative journalist that you got to know people who could find their way round the system. Adam Weston was the kind of geek you needed to know in this profession. Yet care was needed in working with people like Adam. When did the legitimate need to know get trumped by the claim that it was a criminal act to invade privacy? It was getting this narrow distinction right that was success or failure in Miles' world.

He forwarded the message to Weston with the simple message: *Location?*

He would know what to do. The RIM technology in use on his phone meant that even if Miles' phone was under surveillance, this communication would be safe. No wonder governments complained.

All he could do was wait.

Chapter 17

Twelve-year-old Jenny Ravitz couldn't understand why they'd been forced to move. It wasn't fair.

It had been hard to fit in on Mission Bay and now, when she had real friends for the first time, her mother had told her she would have to leave them behind in San Diego. When she'd asked why, the answer had been too pat. "Your father's political interests require him to be in Texas. We're a family that stays together. Real close."

She was old enough to know this was an excuse, adult-speak for not letting her know the real reason why they had to move so suddenly to Austin. "And you don't care if I lose all my friends?"

"Of course I do, dear. But you'll make new ones. A smart and pretty girl like you."

Jenny had gone to her room and cried. She'd moped all the way to Austin. Now, in her bedroom in the apartment overlooking Town Lake, it was no better. A new school to face when term started, if they ever let her leave the house. She would be back to zero in the pecking order.

Something was wrong, though. Her father had never looked this worried. If she'd been asked, she'd have said that both her parents looked scared but no one was asking her. Because they wouldn't let her know what was happening she could only listen and guess.

She could hear them arguing. It was nothing unusual. Her mother and father had been rowing ever since she could remember. Jenny cupped her ear to the wall and listened.

It was her mother. "If your family had never bought it, none of this would have happened."

Her father shouted back. "Let's not go back over all that again. It happened. It brought shame to our family but we lived through it. It's what's happening now that we need to set our minds on."

"And that was enough to mean we had to leave Mission Bay?"

"We're being given the best protection. When they say we're in danger, you have to believe it."

"And what makes you think we're any safer here?"

Her father spoke more softly. Jenny strained to hear. "This place has been chosen carefully. It's a gated compound with high-level security. And we have a couple of extra men watching over us twenty-four seven. Nowhere could be safer."

"So, we can't go out?"

"Not for a while. Just be assured we're not sitting ducks here. I have men out there working to stop this thing before it can get started."

Jenny lay back on the bed. There was so much that her parents were not telling her.

Chapter 18

Wolfgang Heller was back at the *Gambit Hotel* watching the late morning routine unfold. It was better to have returned. He'd hidden the body well and cleaned up professionally but if news of the chef's death broke they would be looking for anyone making sudden movements. In any case, he had one more piece of urgent business to attend to here and he wouldn't move until it was completed.

He wasn't concerned that someone might have seen him. In all the incidents like this in which he'd been involved that was never the issue. He'd learned that the on-site CCTV coverage in most towns took days to process and was of such poor quality that by the time any images were made public he would be gone and would have changed his appearance and the ID he used for travel. He also knew if anyone had seen him their ability to recall his appearance was limited and the computer generated mug shots the police would produce would not look enough like him. It was the on-site evidence – the weapon and the DNA traces – on which modern policing depended and he'd taken care of that.

There was a commotion around the reception desk as the hotel manager struggled with the knowledge that the fat chef had not returned for work.

The blonde waitress was in full flow. "Send someone round to his apartment. He's probably sleeping."

"OK. Open the restaurant for lunch. Serve cold stuff."

"They're not going to like it. I don't want to have to deal with the complainers."

"I'll put up a notice. They'll have to accept it."

Heller shook his head. There it was again – the absence of civility that blighted this town.

He went back to his room and lay on the bed. He'd not forgotten the blonde waitress and her role in what had happened that morning. There had been more than one person's sputum. He couldn't forget that.

He went down to the dining room and read the sign.

> *Due to unforeseen circumstances. A limited midday service.*

Some of the guests were complaining. The blonde waitress was telling them to take it to the manager. When they went to reception they were told he couldn't be found.

Heller didn't complain. He read the notice without comment. He took his seat in the room and ate the cold food. He smiled at the waitress and exchanged a few words with her. He had a polite conversation with the English visitor who told him the visit to the university was a great success.

He knew when the shift ended. He waited for the blonde waitress on her walk home and pushed her into an alley. He broke her neck with a swift movement and let her drop to the floor.

She deserved a quick death. He brought this to all his female victims.

He lifted her up and disposed of her in one of the dozen waste bins crowded together in the alley.

Wolfgang went back to his room and packed the few items he travelled with. Now was the time to move. Urgent business was yet to be done.

He checked out.

He would need a new hotel in a new name. He had the paperwork for that.

Chapter 19

Julia knew something was wrong.

She should never have let James go. He'd been away for more than three hours, leaving her alone in the hotel room.

She tried to find ways to make the time pass. TV made matters worse and the twenty-four hour news reminded her all over again that things were very wrong. There was no mention of a killing in Weymouth let alone the reporting of the death of an FBI man, as she would have expected. She turned the set off.

James. Where are you?

She tried not to think the worst. What if James didn't come back? What if someone discovered she was here and came after her? How would she defend herself?

Being pregnant did not mean she couldn't fight but it would limit what resistance she could make since the overriding need was to protect their child. Nothing could be done that imperilled their son.

She searched the room for a weapon. The best she could find was the pair of nail scissors brought with them on the journey here. It wasn't much of a weapon against anyone determined to harm her.

She could attempt to leave the room, to try to find something in the hotel kitchen that might do a better job but she would be seen long before she could get back to the room and lock herself in.

Or she could do what any sensible person would do and phone the police.

Jim had been so convinced this should not happen. It would be a betrayal of him, she knew, but she was here now alone and she had to think only of the baby.

She stared at the in-room phone. It was old-fashioned and sinister but she knew she had to make the emergency call, no matter how much James would have been telling her not to do it.

As she was about to pick up the receiver and dial, the phone rang. She shot back in terror.

The phone continued to ring.

Who knew this number? It could be someone from the hotel with news about James in which case she knew she had to answer it. What if someone had followed them from Weymouth and they were checking to see if she was here? She couldn't decide what to do.

If there was a chance of finding out what had happened to James, she knew she had to take the call.

Julia picked up the phone.

It was Miles. "Julia. Don't put the phone down. We need to talk."

Miles was the last person she wanted to speak to.

Julia was blocking out the memory of what happened in Florence, she knew that. She was keeping out how she'd suffered at the hands of Alfieri Lando, the disgust she'd felt, the self-loathing on feeling his breath close to her face, the feeling of shame as he touched her, the determination to deny him any sign of response. She was denying the pain that came with each memory, the feelings of dread she knew she must now face.

Was this was the price she had to pay to re-engage, to step off the long, slow slope of recovery and cross over into the immediate uncertainty of recognising the truth of all that had happened in Florence? It was the steepest of climbs back to reality.

It wasn't just the memory of Alfieri Lando. His was an evil so debased and lacking in humanity and, had she not experienced it, she would not have believed its existence. Yet she had to overcome the still-present call of her addiction, inviting her now to sink back into its arms, to luxuriate in its nothingness, to embrace non-being once more. The addiction Lando had forced upon her would remain for the rest of her life as that pale voice whispering to her the necessity of weakness, a demon she had to overcome every bit as terrible as the despair that Lando had brought into her life. She felt she was like her own child to be, bound to emerge yet not wanting to be thrust into the cold, painful light of this cruel day.

Cruel because she knew without having to be told that James was in trouble, not just because it had been so long since she'd heard from him but because she knew deep inside this awful truth was real.

He'd known she was in trouble all those years back and had not failed in his faith in her. Just as he'd found a way to save her, so she must now find a way to save him.

She would be strong and face these demons of her past. This was no longer a matter of choice but of necessity.

She would find the strength to face the threat to herself and her family, to overcome it and get James back.

She lay back on the bed and cried. She told herself, "Julia. You hear me? That's the last time you cry."

Yes, Miles was the last person she wanted to speak to.

"Julia, are you still there?"

These terrible feelings at what had happened in Florence had returned just at the sound of his voice, yet he might know something. "Are you with James?"

There was a pause, too long a pause, before Miles answered. "I waited at Charing Cross but he didn't show. I thought he must be with you."

"He's been gone over three hours. Miles, I'm really worried."

"Then, let's talk."

"How did you get this number?"

"I got someone to hack it for me from the email Jim sent. That's not important. Give me the word and I'll come in."

"OK." Julia could think of nothing else that made sense. With James missing, Miles was her only source of help, no matter how distressing it would be to meet him again.

He was knocking on the door in five minutes. When she let him in he looked older than she recalled. The three years since they'd last sat in a room together hadn't been kind to him. There were lines where the guilt of what had happened in Florence peeped through the untroubled face she remembered.

He spoke first. "I hoped it was going to be easier than this when we met again."

Julia knew it was never going to be easy. But this was worse than she could have imagined. "Tell me about Jim?"

Miles shook his head. He wanted to tell her how sorry he was for having brought so much trouble into her life, for ever having made a connection between her and the Landos, but this wasn't the time. "Julia, there's nothing I can say to make this sound any better. He didn't show."

She was about to cry when she stopped herself. She reminded herself to stay strong to help find James, to stay strong for their child. "Then we have to find him."

Miles moved closer, as if about to comfort her, but her look told him not to come nearer.

He drew away. "Tell me everything that's happened in the last twenty-four hours, beginning with why you're here in London."

When she'd finished she felt no clearer herself about how she and James had been propelled with such haste into this new situation. "Something's triggered this whole thing. And we're on the wrong side of it."

Miles listened in silence. He began to place the events into the kind of framework he used with his investigations for the newspaper. Establish the facts. Corroborate the facts. Make the connections. Draw the conclusions. And right now there was an absence of corroboration that he found worrying.

"Julia, I've not seen anything in the media about an Agent Franks being killed."

She understood what he was implying. "So, you think there's a cover up? I did check when we could still use the iPad. It was reported online on the site of the local Weymouth newspaper."

"And not reported again?"

"You're saying we've been fools to come here."

"I'm not saying that. Just give me time to corroborate this. In my business, I know people who can help find information like this. There's not much information out there that can't be obtained if you ask the right questions."

Julia wasn't impressed. "It didn't help us last time."

"Please don't say that. Let's make our peace with each other some other time. The important thing is to find Jim."

She knew he was right. "OK. How long will you need?"

"Give me an hour."

"I'm still not convinced I shouldn't go to the police."

"Believe me, after what you've told me, I need to tell you I agree with Jim. It's the last thing you should do."

"Then I have to wait here?"

"Trust me. I'll get help as soon as I can."

No matter how hard she tried Julia knew trusting Miles was something that would not be easy.

When Miles left she locked the door behind him. She could only hope that Miles would be true to his word.

Chapter 20

The Land Rover was towed away along with the hundred other vehicles removed from Central London every day and was now in the vehicle pound on Commercial Road in Tower Hamlets.

DI Martin Reid had travelled from Weymouth as soon as he'd seen the report that the vehicle had been found. Once it became clear that what the Harringtons had told him was a lie, he'd set up a marker to have the location of the vehicle sent to him. The address in Edinburgh had been real but when the local police called they found that the occupants – a young couple with three children – had no knowledge of anyone called Harrington.

The couple had left Weymouth in a hurry. Their house was empty. A check with their bank showed the withdrawal of a large sum. They were on the run.

It had not taken Reid long to discover why. These things are supposed to remain secret within the police force but a few enquires amongst colleagues soon revealed the Harringtons to be a witness protection case. It wasn't too surprising that he discovered this without too much effort. The force was required to make sure the couple was safe by sending officers to observe, albeit at a distance. It was inevitable that an increasing number would know the real names – James and Julia Blake. Armed with this information, Reid tracked down a case officer who'd worked in the Hendricks team in London investigating the murder that led to the need for witness protection. Though he said it himself, Reid was now up to speed on most of the relevant facts.

What mattered now was that James and Julia Blake had absconded to London and here was their vehicle.

Reid showed his CID card to the shabby attendant in charge of the vehicle pound. "No. I haven't come to pick up my vehicle. I'm here to inspect this."

He handed the attendant a print out that gave the registration number.

The attendant made slow progress searching through the scraps of paper that amounted to the record keeping system for the place.

Reid was trying not to sound dismissive. "You guys heard of computers?"

The attendant took time to reply. "We're paper here and proud of it. Know where we are. Haven't lost one yet." He searched through more of the sheets. "Here it is. Top floor. Near the exit."

"It's been cracked?"

"No need. The recovery guys were ready to use the usual tools. If the owners of all those expensive vehicles knew just how easy it was to break into them."

Now Reid was feeling impatient and couldn't hide it. "Can I get into it?"

"Yeah, it's wide open. The guy left it unlocked."

Reid walked to the top floor, found the Land Rover, climbed in and began searching. It was clean. In the glove compartment he found the usual junk and used tickets to the theatre and a jazz concert, both in Southampton, but there was nothing to tell him where the Blakes were now.

He returned to the office and the shabby attendant. "When and where was the vehicle picked up?"

The attendant returned to the piles of paper records and began leafing through them. After a further delay that again tested Reid's patience, the correct sheet of paper was produced. "It was towed away from just off the Tottenham Court Road."

"What street?"

"Stephen Street."

Reid knew the area. Before the post in Weymouth, he'd been with the Metropolitan Force. Stephen Street – that would make the search more difficult. There must be a hundred hotels near there but the chances were the Blakes hadn't gone far, not after the long journey to London, not considering Mrs. Blake's condition.

He thanked the attendant who grunted a reply.

Reid set off to find the street where the Land Rover had been abandoned. It would take some time but he would find them if they were, as he suspected, in one of the nearby hotels.

It was curious, though, that Blake had abandoned the vehicle in this way, yet it was understandable. He must have hoped it would be stolen. He'd not allowed for the fact that there are so many law-abiding souls in this town.

Reid knew it should not have been difficult to justify the trip to London with his commanding officer. The Blakes were wanted for questioning, after all, in the investigation into the killing of Agent Franks. But difficult it had been. The information about the death of the FBI man Franks had been amended. What was at first presented as a killing was now being treated as an accident. Franks had been cleaning his firearm when it had discharged, leaving him dead. There would be an inquest but no police investigation. Reid could tell this was a cover-up. That would be better for him. He would have the field to himself. So, he was here on his own account. As far as Weymouth was concerned he was on leave.

He had good reason to be here. He was tired of seeing others with money, real money, who neither deserved it nor respected men like him who worked in a difficult job for what to them was a pittance. They were people with no real skill or knowledge, many, if not all, with shady events in their past or their family's past. He had a real hatred for those who expected that the mere fact they had money would entitle them to make more money. Yes, he was tired of getting by on the low pay the force gave him when those much less able than him had so much.

Reid had used his contacts well, not just to discover what he needed to know about the Blakes and their past but to find out about the money on their heads.

If he was the one to find them and deliver them up, he could collect two million. It would be enough to start a new life somewhere far away from here, somewhere he would not be on the outside looking in on those with all that fast money.

Chapter 21

There are times when you need people like Adam Weston.

He lived alone in a Victorian basement apartment in Pimlico in a space no bigger than a large cupboard once you took away the kitchenette and shower areas. The space was so filled with computers and their peripherals it was difficult to see how he made room for the single couch that turned into a bed.

Miles knocked twice, paused and knocked three times. He felt foolish but this was the way Weston wanted it.

The hacking Weston did was illegal, it was no good pretending otherwise. He worked on the principle that if he entered the target system in a clean manner, stayed for the shortest time and did no damage while he was there, his transgression could remain unnoticed or, at worst, be regarded as trivial. If he was investigated, he'd established a complex web of proxy servers and accounts between himself and the target to deter all but those with the highest level of determination and resources.

Weston had no interest in anything beyond hacking and computing. Miles was busy chasing the deadlines that plagued the journalist's life. They seldom exchanged much beyond the business at hand. In the two years they'd been working together they knew little about each other and preferred it that way.

Miles began. "Thanks for getting me the hotel address."

Weston shrugged. "It wasn't too difficult."

"I have another problem I need your help with."

"Why else would you be here?"

"It's sensitive."

"You've come to the right place."

"FBI."

Weston blinked. The FBI and the State Department were known to the hacker community as the toughest challenges. To get in and get out clean was the most difficult thing. They all knew that. He smiled again. "Cost you."

Miles nodded. "OK."

"Need to take care. May take time."

"I don't have time. We need to do this now."

Miles told Weston what he needed to know about Agent Franks. "He's shot dead in a public place. The local police begin to investigate. There's an early, incomplete story on a local newspaper blog. Then nothing. Someone's sitting on this. I need to know who and why."

Weston was already tapping at the keyboard before him. Code flowed across the computer screen. "This isn't going to be easy."

"You'll find a way."

Weston fell silent as he toiled with the code. He let out the occasional cuss or whoop of delight as the battle to enter the FBI database unfolded. After twenty minutes he leaned back in triumph. "We're in! Does Franks have a first name?"

"Jack."

"So, John?"

"Guess so."

Weston entered the name. "OK, I have the file. John Franks. Recruited straight from college. Looked to have a bright future in the organisation. Early commendations. Then his career went on the back burner. He's solid. Unremarkable. His latest assignment is coded alpha."

"Alpha?"

"It means you can't get to see the details unless you have additional clearance. Which we don't have. Not yet anyway."

"Black ops?"

Weston turned away from the screen and frowned. "Maybe not. Just secret even to most within the organisation."

"So, legit, then?"

"It's too soon to tell. I'll need to dig further." He turned back to the keyboard and continued searching. "What's this?"

"What have you found?"

"A flag. Says this is political. You didn't tell me this thing is political."

Weston began closing down the computer connection. "That's it! I'm out."

"I need more. It's urgent."

Weston sat back in the chair. "It always is. Meanwhile, I've got a skin in need of saving. You know I could be extradited and get thirty years in a US jail for this? If this is political it's a whole other ball game."

Miles shook his head. "But why cut and run now when we're closing in on what we need?"

"Call it a sixth sense. Call it intuition. Call it self-preservation. Call it anything you like. But that was the time to run. They knew we were in there. They were getting ready to come after us."

"You're safe for now?"

"I hope so."

"You'll go in again?"

"I'll let you know."

"Double your fee."

Weston was reluctant but he agreed. "OK. If you really want it this much."

Miles nodded. "I need you to crack the encryption."

"I can't promise anything. I'll give it my best shot. But only when I'm sure it's the right time to go back in there."

"It means a lot."

Miles left without saying much more. He knew if anyone could get the information he needed, Weston was the one.

Chapter 22

Calling on his old contacts in the Met was going to need care, DI Reid was sure of that. True, there was loyalty in the force but like so much else it came at a price. Yet he wasn't about to bring others into the game unless he had to. He wanted the whole two million. He would have to play this down and use his own money.

He was with Billy Smith in the Lamb and Flag, a pub near Charing Cross Police Station in Agar Street where Smith worked as station sergeant. Smith was someone with access to the information Reid needed but without the ambition to enquire too deeply why he would need it.

Reid turned the conversation his way after the expected opening discussion – why he'd been unwise to leave London to spend his life with the farmers of Dorset – had dragged on long enough. "I'm on a divorce case. Private work, you know. Off the record."

"How much you in for?"

"Nothing much. A few thou, that's all. It's more a special for a mate. His wife's playing around. He needs evidence so that when it gets to court she doesn't skin him for half of what he owns."

"Something to show she's in the wrong and puts her in bad light with the court?"

"Yes. So, the thing is, she's here now in London, shacked up with this bloke and I need to know where they're staying. They're in a hotel in Central London, I'm certain of that. I just need to know which one."

Smith took a long, slow sip of his drink. There was money in this if he played this right. "So what are you proposing, Martin?"

"I was thinking they'd be checking in under false names. Looking furtive. Maybe even suspicious. The kind of thing a hotel manager might report."

"And you'd want me to let you know?"

"Exactly."

"Cost you."

"Come on, Billy. I told you I'm not in on this for much."

"But you also said it was more of a special for a mate. So the money can't be the most important thing for you."

"You're a tough one, Billy. How much?"

"Half."

Reid winced. "Eight hundred. You know that's more than fair. It's going to take you not much more than a few minutes here and there to look over the reports that have come in."

They shook hands. Smith's smile showed he was pleased at the prospect of collecting on the deal. "Look, I've got to get away. I'm on duty in half an hour. I'll look through the reports. Let you know when I've got something."

"Make it soon. I need to catch them at it."

"Give me a call in an hour. I should have something by then."

Reid leaned back in his chair when Smith had left. Eight hundred was less than he'd feared – and his old sergeant had gone away thinking he'd driven a good deal.

He ordered another drink and made a silent toast to the loyalty of the Force.

Chapter 23

I didn't make it to Charing Cross even though it was just a short walk to my meeting with Miles.

The black SUV that I'd half-seen following us into London from Weymouth pulled up alongside me as I walked along Raven Street. It had one of those long sliding doors on its nearside. The door opened. Two men jumped out and pushed me into the back. The door closed and I was off the street.

I didn't have much hope that this had been seen, let alone reported. London is like that. For one of the world's most populated cities, it has areas that are almost deserted even during the height of the day and those in the SUV had chosen well.

They were three men with buzz cuts, dark suits and well-kept teeth. FBI.

It was civilised. No one shoved a rag in my mouth or secured my hands with plastic snap-on bands. No one placed a hood over my head. But the black glass windows of the SUV had been treated so light couldn't get in or out. There was no way of knowing where they were taking me.

I had time to complain. "You can't just lift me off the street like this."

They weren't listening. The suit traveling with me in the back of the vehicle had the same answer no matter what my question. "We'll let you know when we get there."

"Where are we going?"

No reply.

We travelled for over a quarter of an hour before stopping. I could hear the doors of a lock-up being opened as the SUV's engine continued to turn over. I guessed we were still somewhere in London. There had been no let up in the sound of heavy traffic and the need to slow down and stop often that was a feature of city driving.

I was led out of the SUV into the lock-up and taken up a wooden staircase to an office on the first floor.

It was the kind of place that had once been run as a business repairing vehicles. The downstairs was where the mechanics worked while, up here in the office, a manager checked they were working and took the telephone enquiries. But the lock-up hadn't been used for that for some years and now served a different purpose.

I was seated, facing a man who looked like Agent Franks but who lacked the hint of compassion I had seen in his face. This face showed only determination.

He spoke clearly with a mid western drawl. "I'm Agent Nate Craven. My colleagues are Agents Michael and Jones. We didn't want to have to bring you here like this but I want you to know we had no choice. You know about Agent Franks?"

"I was told he'd died. Is that true?"

Craven nodded. "A tragic accident. We're doing all we can for his family."

"I don't see how I can help you."

"We need to know why he came to see you."

"You don't know that already?"

"We need to hear it from you."

I told them what I knew about Agent Franks. It wasn't much and they weren't fazed by what I had to say. "So why is there nothing in the media about it?"

Agent Craven was firm. "That's something you can leave to us. We're taking care of it."

"Like you're taking care of me by bringing me here against my will?"

He was trying to sound reasonable but each word he spoke concealed a threat. "Sometimes these things are necessary. For the greater good." He paused and looked over at his colleagues. "That's what we do."

Agents Michael and Jones, standing behind me, just out of my peripheral vision, remained silent.

Craven placed his hands behind his head and linked his fingers to support his ample neck. "Look, James, what Franks said to you still holds. We want your help."

"And, like I told Franks, I can't believe you don't have people more able than me."

"We need you."

"There's nothing you could say that would get me to agree, you must know that."

He smiled. "Nothing?"

"Nothing in this world."

He signalled to Jones who thumped a large paper file onto the tabletop. Craven pushed it towards me. "Take a look at this."

It was about Miles. I leafed through the pages. There were several hundred documents all marked: Secret – Not for Disclosure.

Craven spelled it out. "Your brother's been acquiring information illegally from the State Department. From someone you would call a whistleblower. Top-secret information about US intentions in Mexico and Latin America. Stuff he's been using in his so-called investigative journalism."

Oh, Miles. Where was this leading?

I was suspicious as I cast my eyes over the large volume of material in the file. "If you know all this, I assume you've not wasted time in arresting the informer?"

"That's not necessary."

"You mean you got all this evidence on Miles from a sting?"

Craven smiled. "If that's what you want to call it. Yes, the informer was one of our own, feeding brother Miles non-sensitive information. But you know it makes no difference, don't you? The crime has still been committed."

"How long?"

"What do you mean, James? How long has he been doing this? Or for how long will he be put away? On the first of those questions, he's been at it for over two years."

"You're going to prosecute?"

"That depends on you."

"I have a choice?"

"That's why you're here."

"He's a British subject."

Craven sat up straight and leaned closer. "There won't be a problem with extradition. The US/UK treaty we signed a few years back has already delivered more than once. Those documents your brother has been involved with threaten the security of the State. There's a cast iron case for extradition. We'll try him in Texas. That's the relevant jurisdiction. He'll be lucky to get less than thirty years."

"And if I go along with you?"

"The charges go away."

"This must mean a great deal to you."

"It does."

"How do I know I can trust you?"

"You can trust the FBI."

"You need to do better than that."

"If this thing works out, if you help us as we wish, it will become clear to you why the charges won't need to be laid."

I wanted to help Miles. The thought he could spend that time in a Texas prison was hard to bear. If he came out alive, he would be a broken man.

But Craven had another ace to play.

He was trying to sound conciliatory again. I knew there was worse to come.

"Look, James. I know you're worried about your wife. Who wouldn't be? With the baby coming along so soon."

I could feel rage growing inside me. What right had he to talk about Julia like this and invade my family's privacy? But I knew I had to stay in control.

"That's none of your concern."

"But it is our concern, James. Since it affects the way you feel about the proposition we're making to you. I mean we know how concerned you are about your wife's safety and the wellbeing of your son. Why else would you have run to London?"

I was in no position to protest, but protest I did. "You might think you have the power to do anything you want, but threaten my family and I'll stop at nothing to find a way to stop you."

He held up his hands. "Whoa, James. We're not threatening here. Think about it. So long as Julia stays where she is, we could have her protected twenty-four seven. You wouldn't have to worry about her safety. And you'd have no reason not to agree to help your brother."

"You're offering to protect her?"

He nodded.

They had the two most important people in my life right where they wanted them, three, if you counted our son. There was the direct threat they could get Miles arrested at any time they chose and there was the more than implied threat to Julia if I didn't go along with what they wanted. I knew they could make a move on her at any time. It was the other side of the protection Craven said he was offering.

I determined to stay strong. "I don't buy it."

Craven was disappointed. "I'm not sure I heard that right."

"I don't buy it." I was shouting now. "Look, there's no way I can be certain you're FBI. But that doesn't matter. I'm not a US citizen. You don't have jurisdiction here. Tell me why my best course of action isn't to go to the British police? And why I shouldn't then tell Julia and Miles what you're doing."

Craven made a point of showing me his FBI shield. He asked his two colleagues to do the same. "Don't ever doubt we are who we say we are, James. That would be a mistake."

I had to admit the ID looked genuine.

Craven continued. "And as for going to the local police. Well, I would have thought the two million dollars Matteo Lando has offered for you would be a problem."

I still wasn't convinced. "I'll take my chance. Julia and Miles need to know what a twisted situation this is."

Craven had no need to shout. "James, there's one other thing I didn't mention. What makes you think we're planning to let you go anytime soon?"

Chapter 24

Miles returned to the Allegro Hotel and sought to reassure Julia. "I have a good man, Adam Weston, on the case."

Julia had just one question. "Where's James?"

Miles looked away. He had nothing to say.

"The FBI?"

He looked her in the eye for the first time. "They're covering up the Franks killing. But I need more time to find out why."

"But Franks was FBI?"

"He was, just as he told you. He was involved in some kind of special operation."

Julia could feel a new weight descending on her. It couldn't be coincidence, she was clear about that. The last time their lives had been under threat, Miles had been involved. Now the same threat had returned and here he was, James' ever so helpful brother. If she was ever to see James again, she knew she'd have to go against her instinct to avoid this man at all costs. She knew she would have to enter into his world.

They fell as quiet as two chess players pondering their next move. There was only the distant sound of traffic and the occasional whirring of the hotel elevator to break the silence.

Julia summoned up the courage to speak first. "James told me you've been investigating Alessa Lando?"

"Yes, I told Jim about it, but he wasn't interested. He said it was best left in the past."

"The past. I wish it was just that."

Miles looked away and would say no more.

"How do I know your investigation hasn't led to this?"

Miles took time to reply. "I don't think it has."

"It's down to coincidence, then? You're investigating the Landos and FBI men show up at my house and here I am in London with James missing."

"That's not the connection, Julia. Don't you think I haven't turned it over and over in my mind? The possibility that I might be the reason why harm is being brought to you and Jim again is never far from my thoughts. As if I could ever forgive myself for what happened in Florence. But this is not it. I'm sure of that. Look, I've been investigating Alessa Lando ever since she walked free from the Florence court. That was almost two years ago. If my investigation was the cause, don't you think the Landos would have made a move before this?"

Julia was puzzled. "Then what? Why now? Why the price on our heads?"

Miles looked away. "All I can say is that at a time like this you have to look at what's changed. Something recent must have set this off. It's what all my journalism experience tells me."

"And?"

"There's a line of investigation that I'd discounted. Something I did some work on before deciding it was a dead end. Now I'm not so sure."

"Tell me."

He did not meet her eyes as he looked up. "I was approached by a man who came up to me when I'd just finished speaking at the Investigative Media Congress in San Tropez last month. He knew about me from the publicity surrounding my articles on the Lando's waste dumping. He told me I should be looking into the death of Richard Westland."

Julia cut in. "The Richard Westland?"

Miles nodded.

"He's like a god to a whole generation of young painters. You know he was a key influence on the second Brit Art wave?"

Miles agreed. "So I discovered."

"I know his wife and I met him more than once. He could paint anything. It was my dream that one day I'd get the chance to curate one of his exhibitions. He was a real talent. It was a huge loss when he died in an accident."

"The man at the Congress told me Westland's death was no accident. I asked him why he was telling me this, but he wouldn't reply. On reflection, I think he was scared. But at the time, I took him to be just another one of those types that read what you've written and then invent something to attract attention. He melted back into the crowd. That could have been it, but I had a piece of luck. One of the journalists there recognised the man. I was told he was Alain Bellard. The journalist had covered a court case in France in which Bellard was accused of a string of art thefts."

"He went to prison?"

"No, he was acquitted despite the evidence that he was behind numerous thefts over a thirty year period."

"He must have had a good lawyer."

"Or he bribed the right people."

"So why did he tell you that about Westland?"

"Well, while I wasn't impressed by Bellard, I still did some digging back into the court case, and guess what? Westland was named as an associate of his. There was nothing proven to be illegal but I discovered there was a connection between them going back over thirty years. At the very least there is evidence that the two men moved in the same circles, at least for a while. As you know, Westland was ultra-respectable and well-regarded on his death but back then it may have been different. Thirty years ago, Westland was a struggling artist, as all artists are when they're starting out. The temptation of making some quick money by associating with the likes of Bellard may have been too much for him."

Julia wasn't convinced. "But he was no thief. Why would he have been at all useful to a man like Bellard? Any involvement with art theft and he would have risked his whole future. His career as an artist would have been finished. It would have been unthinkable. And look where his career finished. He became one of the most influential painters of his generation."

"Unless back then he was really desperate. Another contact told me there were rumours Westland had been on the point of bankruptcy at one time but received a last minute bail out. He had no money problems after that."

"But it still doesn't amount to proof."

"Julia, I don't know a single good investigative journalist who works on cast iron proof. There's instinct in this game. And my instinct was telling me to look further."

"So?"

"I looked into Westland's death. It happened just days before Bellard approached me at the convention."

"The crash was an accident."

"I got hold of the coroner report. Westland's vehicle had just been serviced. The garage records showed that the vehicle was passed as being in good working order. Yet the cause of the accident was brake failure. Perhaps the vehicle was tampered with."

"That would be an assumption."

"Unless you're working on cui bono."

"Who benefits?"

"And there's something I haven't yet told you. The reason why Bellard approached me at the conference was that he knew the identity of the person responsible for Westland's killing. I'm sure of it. He wanted to tell me, but something stopped him."

"You didn't take the investigation any further?"

Miles looked away again. "No, Julia. That's the other thing you learn in journalism. When you're trying to crack a story, don't get diverted from the main path. However important it looks, put it on one side if it's not taking you there. And, don't forget, I'm trying to break the Landos over their drugs operation. That's my goal. So, what Bellard might have wanted to say had to wait for another day."

"Until now."

"As I said, Julia, it's one of the things to have changed."

"But you're still not sure?"

"It's there, nagging away. It doesn't fit. I don't like facts that don't fit." He paused. "And, there's something else that doesn't fit. I've just learned that the case Franks was investigating has a political connection."

"What kind of connection?"

"I don't know yet. But believe me, we're doing everything we can to find out."

Julia knew she would not be able to trust Miles again with anything important to her, yet he'd been open and straightforward. She was grateful for that.

She made a decision. "I need to call Peggy Westland."

Chapter 25

No one knew or cared about what happened in Sollicciano, unless you were here for life.

That was Matteo's fate. He'd been born and raised to complete his destiny by killing his father and spending the rest of his days in here.

If only he'd realised soon enough how much Emelia had meant to him. If only he'd been able to dig himself out from under the influence of his father before she'd been killed.

That was in another life. He had this life now and he had a problem to solve – what to do about James and Julia Blake.

He was getting ahead of himself. The key to his problem was to recall how the current situation had come into being. His mother, Alessa, had been placed in danger by actions taken many miles away. She'd told him this related to events thought to be a long way in the past, before she became a Lando. She'd come to him as head of the family for help, even though he was in this place, and he'd known the right man to help in this task.

Wolfgang Heller was the best of Sollicciano. When Matteo was in danger of being killed by those who helped the Rossellinis, Heller had been at his side. Emelia was a Rossellini and they had not forgotten how Matteo had lured her to Florence. How he'd corrupted her. It did not concern them that he'd been acting on his father's instructions because they hated Alfieri as much or even more than they hated Matteo. It had been Alfieri who had driven them out of Florence in the turf war between the two families when Matteo was just a child and it had been Alfieri who would not let matters rest, who had pursued Emelia. Alfieri was gone. They couldn't touch him now. Yet Matteo was here, in Sollicciano and a suitable target for vengeance.

They had driven him down by not killing him at once, though they could have killed him any time they wished. They wanted him to experience a long and fearful death and that had been their mistake.

Heller wasn't known as a compassionate man yet a bond had formed between the German and Matteo. While he was at his lowest and fearing he was about to be killed, Heller had befriended him. When Matteo asked the German why he would put his own life in danger he told him it was a matter of standards and he'd seen enough of Rossellini's hired men to know they were not reliable people. They had insulted him for being German and for talking the way he did. He would do this as much for Germany as for Matteo. Yet it was said by many that Heller had been sent into the prison to protect Matteo out of loyalty to Alfieri Lando, but when asked the German would not admit or deny this.

No one knew much more than that Heller was in Sollicciano for a minor offence. It was said he'd worked as a mercenary in Indochina, had been captured there, imprisoned and tortured before escaping. He'd spent time in Tibet, taking instruction in one of the secret Hindu sects. When asked about that time, he'd not said much other than a few words Matteo couldn't understand about learning to be true to a higher cause. Whatever it was had hardened the man, had given him this sense that people should do right the way he saw it. Matteo didn't know much more about the German's take on life, nor did it matter. Here was a man he could trust. In the world in which Matteo lived that was a rare thing.

Few in the prison thought Heller would do anything other than play the good inmate and wait out the time to his upcoming release at the end of his sentence but Matteo made careful arrangements. He paid good money to the prison officers on their cellblock to ensure no reports were made that might threaten the release.

It took Heller just one week. No one died. The Rossellini henchmen were quieted. No one knew what Heller said or did but the fear he'd instilled in the Rossellini men was plain to see. Their leader came to Matteo to apologise for what was being done against him. Matteo found no difficulties after that in rising up the ladder to the top of the prison hierarchy. As he progressed, he was able to make arrangements for the Rossellini henchmen to be moved elsewhere in the prison. He owed all this to Heller. He thanked him and paid him well. They kept in contact after Heller's release came through.

It was natural that Heller was the man he chose to ward off the threat to his mother and to the wider family. He could think of no one who would serve him better.

Alessa provided the names of the targets. Matteo's informer in the FBI provided the information needed to track them down. One of those targets was the cause of the threat to the Lando family. He didn't know which but it didn't matter. The solution was to silence them all. That would end the story once and for all. There would be no loose ends.

Except he still couldn't decide what to do about the English policeman who was saying he could find James and Julia Blake.

It was personal. Matteo blamed the Blake woman for the death of Emelia. If she'd not attempted to smuggle Emelia away from Florence, Emelia would still be alive today. If her husband had not alerted the police, Matteo would not be here in prison.

A million for each of them was cheap at the price.

Chapter 26

When Martin Reid called back into the Lamb and Flag an hour after the first meeting, Smith was waiting.

Reid ordered two pints and they sat at a table away from the cluster of drinkers at the bar.

The sergeant was edgy. "You have the money?"

Reid handed over the envelope. "As you wanted it. In cash."

Smith glanced inside. "Not that we need to check."

He pulled a similar-looking envelope from his pocket and gave it to Reid. "I hope you get your man."

He pocketed the money and turned away. "I'll be getting back."

"No time for your pint?"

"You know how it is, Martin. It's all about efficiency these days."

"What are you going to do?" Reid glanced at the envelope. "About the names?"

"What can we do? It's not as if they've committed any crime, is it? All that efficiency has left us short-staffed."

Smith stood up and was gone before Reid could say anything more.

It was time to open the envelope. Inside was a print out from the police station database with the names of twelve couples registered in the past twenty-four hours at Central

London hotels where the hotel manager had pointed to suspicion over their status.

The Blakes would know better than to use the Harrington name and they would not want to go by their real names either, which meant they would have a problem with proof of identity. Reid searched through the stated reasons for suspicion, looking for those mentioning issues with ID. The list of possibles reduced to four.

He stretched out his legs beneath the table.

Time to enjoy his pint.

Smith had told him there was no risk of anyone from the station following up on the listed names. Reid had the scene to himself.

It would not take long to check out all four hotel addresses.

All were in a one-mile radius.

Chapter 27

It wasn't going to be easy but Julia knew she had to do this.

She'd met Peggy Westland many times in her work as a conservator. Peggy had often called in at the Clinton Ridley Restoration Studio. She had a genuine interest, not just because her husband Richard had been one of the most important abstract painters in the land but also because she was a perceptive art critic in her own right.

Julia had no idea how Peggy might be coping with the loss of Richard. Though she must be taking it hard, Julia had to overcome any restraint. Finding James was her overriding priority.

She got the number from the enquiry company and prepared to dial. It was best to sound untroubled, she knew. Given how she felt, this wasn't going to be easy, either. She dialled.

The call was picked up straight away. Peggy Westland sounded angry. "If this is a cold call of any kind you're out of luck."

"It's no cold call, Peggy."

"That's what they all say."

"It's Julia. Julia Blake."

It was the first time she'd used her real name in three years. It sounded strange. Yet if the cover was blown, if the new identity had been cracked, it would be no safer calling herself Mary Harrington.

"Julia, I'm sorry. You must know how I am. Losing Richard."

"I'm sorry for your loss, Peggy. Please accept my sincerest condolences."

"It's been a while."

"I'm sorry we couldn't make the funeral. My recovery…"

"I know. I know what you went through. It's good to have you back."

Julia needed to move the conversation on. "Look, Peggy, I know this will be difficult for you, but I need to ask you some questions about Richard's work."

"You already know how important he was. You've already seen most of his work. You can read my critical articles on the paintings. They're all online. What more could I tell you?"

"I need to know about his relationship with Alain Bellard."

Julia could hear the intake of breath on the other end of the line. "That name means nothing to me."

"It's from when Richard was a young struggling artist, the best part of thirty years ago. Perhaps you could cast your mind back."

Peggy's voice became hostile once again. "Why are you doing this? Don't you have any sensitivity? Raking over the past at a time like this."

"I know it's hard for you, Peggy but…"

"But nothing! Tarnishing Richard's reputation before he's cold in the ground. I don't need this."

"I need to know."

"What, so that brother-in-law of yours can publish another of his investigative articles? I'd have thought even he wouldn't have sunk as low as to put you on to me to flesh out a story."

Julia bit her lip. "I'm not working for Miles. I'm trying to save my husband."

"James?"

"I think they have him."

"They?"

"I don't know who they are, but he's missing and the only thing I have is this connection to Bellard and your husband. You have to help me. I'm sure his life's in danger."

There was a long pause. Peggy Westland was thinking long and hard before making her next reply. "I understand. But I can't be a part of destroying Richard's memory. His legacy. You know, it took years of hard work and dedication for him to be recognised as the great artist he is… He was. I can't do or say anything to imperil that. It's what I have left."

Julia knew she had to get this right. "I promise you, nothing you say will be used to tarnish your husband's memory. I'm only interested in getting James back. Did Richard ever know Bellard?"

There was a further long silence, broken by Peggy in a voice that was almost a whisper. "He knew him. He confided in me. He told me it was the only way of getting out of his money troubles. Bellard was a bad influence. He introduced him to people who were making money out of art in an illegal way. He told me all he had to do was to paint like Picasso. And he could do that without having to think about it."

"And what good was that to Bellard?"

Peggy Westland sighed. "He never told me. But I don't think Bellard was the brains behind it."

"Who, then?"

"I really don't know. It was a long time ago now. It's a part of Richard's life buried in his past. One I was sure would remain that way."

"You don't have another name? Anyone else your husband may have been associated with back then?"

"It really was so long ago. The only other name I can give you is Pugot. Marcel Pugot. He was an art dealer with a gallery in Ghent. Richard went out there to meet him on a few occasions. He was somehow involved along with Bellard but that's all I can tell you."

"You say 'was'?"

"Pugot died. Just three weeks before Richard. Though he tried to hide it from me, it had a bad effect on Richard. But that's all I know. He wouldn't confide in me any further."

Julia realised she'd pushed Peggy Westland as far as she could. "Peggy, you've been very helpful. I'm sorry to have troubled you. I hope I won't have to bother you again. Please accept my condolences once more."

After Julia ended the call, she looked over towards Miles who'd been listening. "She pointed me to an art dealer named Marcel Pugot from Ghent in Belgium. He died three weeks ago. What can we find about him?"

Miles replied, "I'll ask Weston to get onto it." He paused. "Look, I have to leave. You have my number. Keep the door locked. If you need anything, just call. I'll call back here tomorrow at nine."

Julia phoned room service and ordered her evening meal. It would seem strange eating without James.

Chapter 28

Miles returned to Adam Weston's apartment and was let in.

"You have something?"

Weston looked contrite. "I don't have much to tell you. But you need to know right up front, I haven't been able to crack the alpha coding."

Miles wanted to make sure. "The FBI encryption is too strong?"

"It's too complex. I might as well be straight with you. I can't stay in there long enough to get a decent crack at it, not without getting caught. I need to be ultra-careful. It's going to take much longer than I thought. Sorry."

"Time is what we don't have."

"I know that. I'll push on as hard as I can."

Miles thanked him. "We have another lead. Something that could be easier. Marcel Pugot from Ghent."

"How do you spell that?"

"Ghent in English. Gent if you're Flemish."

"No, the name."

Miles spelled it out. "Marcel Pugot. An art dealer."

"I can try. What do you need?"

"As much as you can find. Anything linking him to a British painter named Richard Westland."

"And the connection?"

"That's what we're looking for."

"Anything else to go on?"

"Just that both have died in the past weeks."

Weston's screen was filling with scrolling code as he typed in instructions to his computer at great speed. "I guess the best place to start would be the Belgian national police database. Let's see."

"Nothing as difficult as the FBI database?"

Weston smiled. "Maybe not. I'm in. What do you want to know?"

Chapter 29

They drugged me and put me on a military plane out of RAF Brize Norton.

It was a kind of rendition.

I shook myself awake. I had no idea how much time had passed since we'd left London.

Craven was somewhere up front. The men he introduced as Agents Michael and Jones when I was questioned at the lock-up were traveling with him. They were huddled together, talking as a team, no doubt making plans that concerned me but I couldn't hear what they were saying above the drone of the aircraft.

Others had joined them – I counted eight, including the one they'd left to watch over me. He said his name was Philips.

He was making a point of not answering my questions.

"How long was I out for?"

"Long enough."

"Where are you taking me?"

"Don't worry, buddy. It's not that far."

"So, where?"

"You'll find out soon enough."

Philips was lying. It didn't feel like we were anywhere near London. In fact, from the appearance of those around me, it looked as if we'd been traveling a long time. That meant, in all probability, we were no longer in Europe.

I was having trouble understanding how these people could have this much power over me and have such disregard for the law. I knew what Craven would say if I asked him. "*We are the law.*"

My thoughts were centring on how Craven and his men could command such resources – the use of military transport to fly me out of London, the covering up of the Franks killing. They must be who they say they are. They must be FBI.

This meant only one thing. They must be black ops. No straight FBI operation would be carried out like this.

Could I believe what Craven said before we left London?

Could I believe anything he told me?

All the time, with every mile the plane travelled, I was being taken further away from Julia.

That meant more than my own safety.

Since I couldn't trust what Craven had told me, there was no way of knowing if Julia was safe.

The thought would not go away.

Day 3

Wednesday August 21ˢᵗ

Chapter 30

Julia came round from disturbed sleep.

It was early morning. The baby was kicking. This must be what had woken her. She hugged her belly. *It is going to be all right. Pretty baby, there's nothing to worry about.*

She'd been dreaming – a nightmare. Painful though it would be she knew it was important to recall it all.

The dream had taken her back to Florence, a place she did not want to see again, to the house in Lucca where she'd worked on the Lando painting collection, all the time unaware of what was to come. How natural and satisfying and uneventful it had all seemed then, searching through the paintings, deciding which ones to investigate.

She shuddered.

Seeing Alfieri Lando coming towards her, dressed in the mask and cape that he wore to defile Emelia and then defile her, came as a shock. There was a glimpse, too short, of Emelia's face. The sister she hadn't known for all her life and who was lost to her so soon after she'd found her was taken away from her all over again.

Next came a fractured image of a woman's face. Julia felt the anguish of imagining the woman's grief at what she'd seen and saw her tears. Tears that told of the suffering of the whole of humanity, ice white against green, yellow, blue and red primary colours. The woman's hands held up to her face as if to say she should not look at the horror before her any longer. Her features etched out in broad lines of black while the eyes continued their icy stare, unable to look away. There would be no relief from the necessity of testifying to the horror. In her dream it was a face not unlike a distorted version of her own.

Yes, it was a nightmare, one that had not ended even though she was now wide-awake.

The simple wonder of being here in the bed in the hotel with her baby moving inside her was what she knew she must hold onto as a way back from the terror that pervaded her.

Her prime sense of purpose returned. Her baby. She knew she must eat again. Room service would take too long. She decided to brave the hotel restaurant.

She washed, dressed and put on her face.

It was never easy eating alone and less easy when pregnant. Unlike the day before when she'd been with James, the waitress made a great show of making her comfortable when on any objective account she was finding the best way of making Julia less noticeable, seating her at a table in a corner on the furthest side of the restaurant from the door.

Breakfast was slow in coming, and poor, yet Julia was grateful for the anonymity of the place. When she began to eat she realised how hungry she was and how her baby must have been waiting for the rush of nutrients he so needed.

The meal was interrupted by the arrival of the hotel manager. He sat opposite without being asked and spoke in too-quiet tones. "Mrs. Meredith. Do you have the identity documents I requested when you checked in?"

Julia lied. "My husband has them."

"And where is your husband? He's not been seen in the hotel since a few hours after you arrived."

"He's been called away. On business."

"Then how can he provide me with the proof of identity?"

"He'll be back later tonight. I'll send him down to you with them. You said forty-eight hours."

"OK, this evening at the latest." The manager left Julia to finish the meal. She was angry with herself that she had not found a way past this.

Julia went back upstairs and was alone again in the room. Though she tried to place her mind elsewhere, she was drawn back to recalling the nightmare that had woken her and the terror of being back in Florence again. The fractured-face woman weeping for the tragedy around her in the world returned and she couldn't get the image out of her mind.

Julia could see it clearly. The image of the woman was not a distorted version of herself as she'd supposed when she first recalled the dream. It had come to life from a painting. It was a picture she could now identify. It was Picasso's *Weeping Woman*, his representation of his lover Dora Maar, revealing to the world her grief at the mutilation of souls at Guernica.

There was something more, something she'd seen while in the Lando house and was now repeated in the dream, something important that she'd blocked out along with so much more she'd attempted to forget on the long road to recovery.

It was one of a number of paintings she'd seen when selecting the pictures from the Lando collection for her studies. It had been hidden behind a panel that had opened to her touch. It was something she was not supposed to have seen.

She closed her eyes. The painting she'd seen was Picasso's *Weeping Woman*. It was in the dream because she'd seen it for real in the Lando house in Lucca.

It was a near-perfect copy of the original. You could almost believe it was the real thing.

Those memories that Julia had buried were now rushing back and with them came questions that had remained unanswered for three years as she'd been drawn into the trap set for her by Alfieri and the darkness that had entered her life then and remained with her now. Why would Alessa Lando allow her vanity to go beyond the mere collection of valuable artworks and into the realm of believing she owned such a masterpiece?

And now she had a new question needing an answer.

Why did Alessa Lando have that painting?

The realisation came as something she should have known all along but which now, out of the act of remembering the dream, formed itself with a solidity that startled her.

Alessa Lando would not have had the painting unless the original had been stolen.

The theft of the Picasso was a major news story all of thirty years ago yet it was an event still talked about in the gallery and conservation circles in which she worked.

She should have felt elated at recalling this important information but her thoughts turned without warning to something she couldn't hope to contain – the possibility of losing James.

The deepest sadness was closing in on her.

She needed fresh air.

Outside on the pavement the rain was just stopping. A cool breeze washed over her as she walked.

She knew she must find a way back to James.

Chapter 31

DI Reid found the Allegro Hotel after drawing a blank at the first two hotels he visited.

The Polish receptionist went straight to summon the manager as soon as she saw Reid's CID card.

The manager was helpful. "Yes, I'm pleased to give you any information you need, Inspector. After the recent outrages no-one can be too careful."

Reid smiled. "Very responsible, sir. John and Elizabeth Meredith. They're staying here?"

The manager checked the computer. "Room 318. No ID. No credit card. No vehicle. Paying cash. I thought you'd need to know. So, I filed the report, as we're requested to do."

"Very good. Very responsible. Any reason why you offered them a room? Why didn't you turn them away?"

"Normally, of course we would. That's company policy. But the woman looked distressed. And she's visibly pregnant."

Reid knew this was the one. He'd observed Julia Blake on his visit to the house in Weymouth. How many pregnant women with no ID have checked into Central London hotels in the past twenty-four hours?

Still, he knew he should not abandon his normal, careful approach. With stakes this high it was important to get it right. "I'd be grateful if I could review your security camera records."

The manager was keen to oblige. "Of course, follow me."

Reid was led to the back office where a large TV screen sectioned into six showed the feed from the hotel's various security cameras. Below this sat the recorder. The feed Reid was interested in covered the reception area. He rewound the recorder twenty-four hours and watched the images stream by at ten times normal speed.

It could have taken hours but luck was on his side. He soon found what he wanted. There they were, James and Julia Blake checking into the hotel.

He'd found them.

It was time to get serious about how he intended to collect on the two million.

Chapter 32

It had gone nine. Julia returned to the hotel to meet Miles.

As she walked through the lobby she noticed the hotel manager showing someone into the back office. Something about their body language gave this the appearance of official business but she could only see the tall man with the manager from behind and let the moment pass.

She hurried to her room to find Miles seated in an armchair on the nearby landing.

"How long have you been waiting?"

He stood up. "A few minutes, that's all."

Julia used her key card to open the door and let him in. She closed the door behind them and tripped the security lock.

"We need to talk."

Miles waited.

"I need ID. Can you help?"

"I'll get someone onto it."

"We're going to need a photo. I've got an old one in my bag." She rummaged in the bag and gave it to him. "It's three years old. One of the ones we didn't use for the Harrington passport. It should do."

Miles glanced at the photograph before placing it in his wallet. "You look as good as ever."

Julia would have accepted the compliment but she did not want to trust Miles even with this.

"I don't have a photo of Jim."

"We'll sort that out when we get him back."

Julia was quick to understand what this implied. "So, there's no word on Jim?"

Miles shook his head.

She had determined to put aside her fears and move on. "Pugot, then?"

"Yes. There's more from Adam Weston. It was straight-forward to get into the Belgian police database."

"And?"

"Pugot wasn't killed. He died in an accident. He was knocked down by a vehicle when crossing the street."

"Do you believe that – Pugot, then Westland? It's too much of a coincidence."

"I'm sorry, Julia, it's a stone-cold case of accidental death. A mother, Amilie Couthard, was driving her children to nursery. The children, buckled up in the rear seats behind her, wouldn't stop crying. She turned round to quieten them and took her eyes off the road for a second but that was enough. She collided with Pugot as he crossed the road. He was flung in the air and came down on the pavement kerb. His skull was fractured. Madame Couthard is remorseful and is facing charges of driving without due care and attention. You couldn't contrive a situation like that. Pugot's death was an out-and-out accident."

Julia shook her head in recognition of what he was saying. "OK, so where does that leave us?"

Miles was in no doubt. "The main point is that when Bellard tracked me down at the convention both Pugot and Westland were dead. No wonder he looked scared."

"There has to be more on Pugot?"

"There is. When Weston got into Pugot's records he found that the much-respected art dealer had been arrested on suspicion more than once by the Belgian police."

"Suspicion of what?"

"Dealing in forged art works."

"Anything from thirty years ago when we know Richard Westland was involved with him?"

"Yes. They'd charged him once back then but the prosecution hadn't stuck. He was acquitted on a technicality. The police collected evidence against him by tapping his phone but they hadn't taken the trouble to get a magistrate to approve the tap. Pugot's lawyer had the evidence ruled inadmissible and Pugot was acquitted."

"So, despite the fact that Westland became one of the most highly-regarded artists of his day, back then, he could have been involved in forgery with Pugot?"

"We don't have proof, not yet, but as you said, Julia, Westland could paint anything."

"And his wife, Peggy, told me there was a link between the three of them, between Westland, Pugot and the art thief Bellard. What kind of paintings were in Pugot's gallery when he was arrested back then? Did the Belgian police files have details?"

Miles nodded. "Modern stuff. Picasso. Braque. Matisse."

"Does the record mention specific paintings?"

Miles shook his head. "We couldn't find that information. Maybe it hasn't survived."

Julia smiled. "Westland was good at the modern masters. They were his biggest influences."

"So, let's say Westland made forgeries for Pugot."

"He would never have called them that."

"Copies then?"

"Yes, copies. Just what was it about them that would get Westland killed? The paintings he made must be relevant."

Miles had still not given up on the scepticism that made him a good investigative journalist. "Maybe it's a possibility, even a likelihood, but it doesn't get us any closer to understanding what's happening now, why you and Jim are on the run, why Jim's missing."

At the renewed thought of not knowing where James was, Julia could feel despair returning despite her best attempts to shut it out. "No, it doesn't. And, yes, it's true, I don't know where Jim is."

She was struggling to avoid crying now. "You're right. There's a missing piece. Something important that set this whole thing off and we don't know what that is. It's something about Pugot and the paintings, I'm sure of it."

Miles wanted to comfort her but knew he had to keep his distance. "I'll get back to Weston. I'm sure he can find more."

"I think Peggy Westland knows more. She took a long time to tell me anything about Pugot and I'm sure she was holding back. She told me Westland went out to Ghent more than once back in the early days and that he was shaken to hear of Pugot's death but she wouldn't elaborate.

I need to see her, face to face and get her to tell me what she wasn't prepared to say over the phone."

Julia picked up the phone and called Peggy Westland. "It's me, Julia. I promised I wouldn't bother you again, Peggy, but James is still missing. I don't know where to turn."

"There's been no news?"

"I need to see you. Can I come over?"

"I've told you all I know."

"Can I come over anyway?"

Peggy Westland conceded. "All right, if you think it will help."

Miles whispered, "I'll drive you."

Chapter 33

We landed at a deserted airport outside of Huntsville. I was loaded into an SUV and taken to Walls Unit, the correction facility.

I tried to tell the guards at the admission station that I should not be here.

The lead officer shoved me against a wall. "If you weren't saying that, we'd surely have the wrong man."

He had more to say. "Harrington, Charles. Not so many calling themselves Charles these days. Can't see that helping you in here."

His colleague gave a toothless smile. "Tough times ahead, Charlie."

"You can't do this."

"Yeah, he's the right guy."

There were smiles all round. "We're just kiddin', right. You're here to look around."

Agent Craven appeared. "Yes, he's on a prison visit with me."

He took me through three sets of locked and barred doors and into a viewing room where we watched as an incoming prisoner was showered and deloused. His head was shaved and he was in an orange jump suit and banged up in an isolation cell in no time with no one to listen to his complaints. The cells, like the rest of the place were nineteenth century and frightening.

Jet lag closed in and I fought not to give in to it.

How did these people have the power to bring me here like this?

How had I become this far separated from Julia that I could no longer protect her?

As we toured the cellblock, Craven took pride in letting me know that Walls Unit was known for having executed over four hundred since capital punishment was restored in Texas back in 1982.

From the cells there was no protest as we passed. Those inside this place were long past any hope that their complaints might be heard.

Craven paused as we were about to leave. "Why did we bring you here? We thought you should get used to the idea that we're serious. This is what brother Miles will get. Each day like this for thirty years. Think about it."

"I'm thinking."

"You now want to play ball?"

I nodded. "Tell me what you want."

"OK. Let's get out of here. Then we'll talk."

The lead officer didn't show much pleasure as he unlocked the exit. I could hear him complaining under his breath to his colleague. "Must be a special. No one tells us a thing. Bring them in. Send them straight back out. Who gives a damn?" Then something for Craven to hear. "And we never got the chance to give him a decent haircut." There were more smiles.

I caught sight of myself reflected in a nearby window. The after-effects of the drugs and the military transport across the Atlantic had not yet worn off and made me look desperate. I doubt if even Julia would have recognised me.

It wasn't long before I was back in the SUV, heading back to the military airport.

Chapter 34

Julia called into the florist in the rear of the Peter Jones store in Sloane Square.

Miles stayed with his vehicle, saying he'd drive round until she'd finished.

The way the florist was stocked made no disguise of the fact that their main business was providing bouquets of condolence – lilies, chrysanthemums, gladioli, carnations. It was unremarkable when you considered the ageing, wealthy population of the immediate area.

Julia wanted something less solemn, something respectful, yes, but holding out hope of future happiness. She chose a dozen long stemmed red roses.

She waited in Symons Street until Miles came past to pick her up again. They drove the short distance to Peggy Westland's smart apartment overlooking a square in Wilbraham Place. Miles parked and wished her good luck. "I'll stay here."

There was a long wait for a reply when Julia pressed the button on the aged intercom. She couldn't help thinking Peggy Westland had decided to avoid her after all, but then came the crackle of the call being picked up inside. She spoke into the receiver. "Peggy. It's Julia Blake."

There was a whir of the electronic bolt as the outer door opened. Julia stepped inside the entrance hall and made her way up a flight of stairs to the apartment. Peggy Westland opened the door before Julia had time to ring the bell. "Come in, my dear."

Julia handed over the bouquet. "Thanks for seeing me. I'm sorry to trouble you again and I know I promised I wouldn't do this."

Peggy accepted the roses with a smile. "You shouldn't have. They're beautiful."

Julia followed her into the kitchen where Peggy unwrapped the roses, laid them out on a counter and searched for a suitable vase. She chose a valuable-looking Art Deco vase and began using scissors to trim the rose stems to the right length. "I did tell you. There's nothing more I can add about Richard."

Julia sat on a chair at the kitchen table. "James is still missing. He's not been seen since he went to meet Miles at Charing Cross. That was over twenty-four hours ago. I need your help."

"What makes you think I can help? Have you been to the police?"

"I can't go to them."

"Why ever not?"

Julia had a decision to make. If she was going to get anything more useful from Peggy than she'd revealed over the phone, Julia would have to take her into her confidence. There were risks. She didn't know how far she could trust Peggy yet there was no choice but to take that risk. "You heard what happened in Florence?"

"Some of it. A murder, wasn't it?"

"More than one. And, worse than that, I was kidnapped and raped."

Peggy stopped arranging the roses. "Oh, my dear, I had no idea."

"It's something I have to live with."

"You're being very brave in telling me this."

"I thought you'd need to know, to help understand the situation Jim is in. That I'm in." Julia paused. She took a deep breath. "The same people who kidnapped me then are involved again now, I'm sure of it. There's some feud, something from the past that's come back to threaten us and I think Marcel Pugot is central to it. Can you please think back to what Richard told you about him? Why did Richard need to visit him?"

Peggy abandoned work on the roses and came to sit on the chair facing Julia. "Then, this is more serious than I thought."

Julia reached forward and held Peggy's hand. "You will help?"

"You know my feelings about the risk to Richard's reputation. You promised me nothing would be said or done that could result in his life's work being ruined."

"Look, I promise with all my heart I'll do everything in my power to avoid that. He was a great artist, an inspiration to me. There's no reason why I'd want to say or do anything to harm his reputation now."

Peggy fell silent. She paused. It was clear she was weighing with great care what to do next. Then, having made up her mind, she stood and went from the kitchen to the dining room. She opened the bureau drawer and removed a plain envelope.

She passed over the envelope. "I wasn't going to show you this. Richard unearthed it from where he'd been keeping it when he heard what had happened to Pugot.

He told me it was their insurance policy, something that would keep them safe."

Julia took the envelope. It was addressed to Richard Westland and carried a Belgian stamp. The postmark was dated 30.11.1983. Julia opened it and removed a single sheet of paper. She read it with care.

> *From Van De Baere solicitors, Gent*
> *To Richard Westland, or the members of their family*
>
> *My name is Marcel Pugot You will perhaps remember me as the dealer who sold you the painting.*
>
> *I no longer have to apologise to you since you will only be reading this letter if l am no longer with you, but apologise I will. I did not intend any harm to you or your family. It was business. Just business. I hope you will accept this.*
>
> *My purpose in writing is straightforward. I want you to know who was responsible in the deception, who planned the theft of Picasso's Weeping Woman and the means of fooling you and others into thinking that the fake I sold you was the real thing. That person was Alessa Lando.*
>
> *You should know you have received this letter on instruction of my solicitor that it should be sent only in the event of my death.*
>
> *Yours*
> *Marcel Pugot*

Peggy Westland spoke first. "I thought you'd know what it means."

Julia found it difficult to reply. Here it was. The key she'd been searching for. The reason for the threats against her, against James and her family.

"Yes, Peggy. I know exactly what it means. Thank you. Thank you for showing it to me."

Chapter 35

DI Martin Reid watched Julia Blake leave the Allegro Hotel.

He admired the Blake woman's courage in getting out and about in her condition. He smiled. She should be that much easier to follow.

Who was that with her – not her husband James?

The inspector's hopes were raised at the thought of the double payment he would claim for delivering them both but it wasn't the husband, even though the man she was with was enough like him. He wondered if Blake had a brother and checked into the Metropolitan police database from the laptop beside him on the front seat of his vehicle. Yes, there was a brother by the name of Miles who worked as an investigative journalist, no less, meaning care would be needed. Reid wasn't disappointed – perhaps they were about to lead him to the husband.

He followed them to the Peter Jones store in Sloane Square and waited in Symons Street as the Blake woman went inside while the driver circled round. Reid was near enough to pick her out when she returned to the vehicle yet not too close to be spotted.

A traffic warden came up. Reid wound down the driver window.

"You're not allowed to park here, sir."

The inspector held up his identity card. The warden glanced at it, winked and walked away.

Reid followed the Blakes the short distance to Wilbraham Place. He watched as she left the vehicle and walked towards one of the apartment blocks.

He weighed up Blenheim Mansions. It was posh. More than posh, it was wealthy. He used the camera with the telephoto lens to photograph the Blake woman as she pressed the bell to request entry into the building. He watched as she was let in.

He downloaded the photograph to the laptop and enlarged the image.

He muttered to himself. "Number six."

He logged back onto the police database, called up the Electoral Register for the area and typed in 6, Blenheim Mansions, Knightsbridge.

Back came the names. "Richard and Margaret Westland."

He returned to the police database. "Richard Westland. Recently reported killed in a road accident. That explains the flowers."

Reid pondered the significance of the visit. Was she consoling a family friend? He doubted that. If you were on the run you would not make such a visit unless it was essential, something important enough to make it worth the risk of being seen.

His optimism rose once more. Perhaps this was where they were hiding James. Yes, that could be it; they could have split up and were using the brother to protect the woman while the husband tried to make sense of what was happening. Reid had no way of knowing if this was the case or not. He would have to visit the apartment to find out for himself.

All he could do now was wait.

Here was the Blake woman leaving the apartment and walking back to the brother's vehicle after just twenty minutes. It wasn't much of a visit.

He followed them into Oxford Street where the traffic slowed almost to a stop.

A delivery van that had been between them pulled over to unload. Reid was right behind them now. He was concerned to be this close. This was not good following practice. If she looked round she might recognise him, but that wasn't going to happen since the Blake woman was preoccupied and was doing most of the talking. He wished he could hear what she was saying. Brother Miles would be able to see him in the driver mirror if he'd cared to pay attention but that wouldn't matter, not in the short term, anyway, as they had never met.

Chapter 36

Miles was ready and waiting when Julia returned. "Get in, please. I'm over the parking limit."

Julia climbed in. Miles started the engine and pulled out into the traffic. "Was Peggy Westland helpful?"

"She took some convincing but in the end I got her to open up to me. It's just as I thought, what's been happening to us does go back to Pugot's death. That's what set off this whole chain of events."

"Even though he died in an accident?"

Julia spoke slowly to emphasise each word. "Yes. It doesn't matter how he died, just that he died. It was enough. Peggy Westland showed me a letter from Marcel Pugot's lawyer, a copy of which was posted to Richard Westland thirty years ago. Richard called it their insurance."

"Insurance for what?"

"In case anything went wrong. In case Alessa Lando tried to remove any loose ends."

Miles pulled out to overtake. "I don't understand."

Julia continued. "It's what the letter is all about. It's not addressed to anyone in particular. It's a form letter that could be sent to any number of people if the opening was changed."

"And Pugot asked his lawyer to prepare such a thing?"

"It says in the letter that it's only being sent in the event of Pugot's death. And, what's more important, the letter names Alessa Lando as being behind the theft of a painting by Picasso. That's what lies behind the threat against James and me. It's not about drugs or any of the crimes you'd expect the Landos to be involved with. It's a thirty-year-old crime about a stolen painting, *Weeping Woman*. Picasso painted half a dozen canvases of the same subject and they're in museums all around the world. I know the one in Melbourne and there's one here in London in the Tate Modern. They're all masterpieces, all worth millions. I'm certain the one they stole was from a small gallery in Hagedet in France. Back then, in 1983, the theft was in all the newspapers and even made the TV."

"It was a long time ago."

"But, don't you see, the time scale fits. I'm convinced that back then Richard Westland was asked to make multiple copies of *Weeping Woman* and they were sold as the real thing to a number of people. Otherwise you wouldn't need a form letter. You'd have a single letter addressed to the person concerned. The lawyer must have been given a list of names to send the letter to. When Pugot died, the lawyer was instructed to send the letter to all those who had been cheated into buying a copy of the painting. That's why they called it their insurance. Pugot must have told Alessa that if she moved against them, the letters would be sent. Her cover would be blown."

Miles was sceptical. "If that was their insurance, it didn't work too well. Westland was killed. What little investigation I had time to do showed that the crash wasn't an accident."

"It kept them safe for thirty years. Don't forget, West-land died after the Pugot letter was sent. That's the real irony. Though Pugot died in an accident, the letters were still sent out by his lawyer. There was no fail safe in the instructions. Pugot may even have wanted the families to know after his death."

"So, they didn't sell the Picasso original?"

"No, Westland made the copies and Pugot sold each copy as if it was the original. The real Picasso was found six months later in a railway station left luggage locker."

"Do we know how many they cheated?"

"It could be five or six, maybe more. We don't know but we do know the type of people they are. They're indi-viduals or their surviving families who've been wealthy enough and foolish enough to buy a stolen Picasso thinking it was the real thing."

"And the letter Peggy Westland showed you is key."

"Yes, that's what sets off the current chain of events, beginning with Pugot's death. The Landos have no reason to hold back once the families know. The Landos are open to retribution themselves – legal action or something less pleasant. I know Alessa Lando. She wouldn't wait. She'd want to get in first and clean up the loose ends."

Miles stumbled upon the key question. "I still don't understand. Why were James and you drawn into this?"

"It's not about James. It's about me. I saw the painting. In Lucca. Picasso's *Weeping Woman*. One of the Picasso copies that Alessa used to cheat those people into thinking they were buying an original."

"I thought she only collected old masters."

"It was there. Hidden. Out of place. And I saw it. A near-perfect copy. Why would she have it? And why would she keep it hidden?"

"Did they know you'd seen it?"

"I don't know. Something changed her attitude towards me. One day everything was fine, the next she wanted me out. They came up with some excuse that I'd been planted there to spy on them, to gather information to do with tax evasion or stolen art, but I don't think it was the real reason. I think now it was because I'd seen something I shouldn't and they'd got to know about it. I'll never know for sure. But what's important now is that I did see the copy of *Weeping Woman*. A convincing copy. One Richard Westland must have made. And you see what that means?"

"Tell me."

"It means I'm one of the loose ends that Alessa Lando needs to clear up."

They were stuck in slow-moving traffic along Oxford Street. Miles was unfazed. "This is going to take some time."

Julia stretched her arms. "Then I have time to tell you I know how Alessa Lando cheated those people. She worked a swindle that had been worked long ago with classical art."

Miles was confused. "Whoa! I don't get the connection. Westland, Pugot, the stuff they were involved in was all modern art."

"You're right, the Landos collected classical art. That's what so bewildered me when I caught sight of the Picasso copy in Lucca. What was it doing there, hidden away in a place I wasn't supposed to know about? And guess what else I found hidden away in the same place as the Picasso – a very good copy of da Vinci's *Mona Lisa*."

"Also by Westland?"

"No, it's not the kind of thing he would have known how to paint. And besides, it looked much more than thirty years old. It looked almost as good as the real thing."

"You saw both in Lucca?"

"Yes, but I've only just been able to put the pieces together now. You know how bad things were there for me, how I've had to shut most things out. Those last few days in Florence are still a blur to me even now. There's still more coming back in flashes."

Miles shifted in the driver's seat. He knew he was close to the moment he feared when he would have to make his peace with Julia over those events in Florence, but the time wasn't right. He sought to move the conversation on. "The *Mona Lisa* alongside the Picasso?"

Julia nodded. "You see, the way Alessa Lando made the theft of the Picasso pay has everything to do with what happened when the *Mona Lisa* itself was stolen."

She brushed a strand of hair from her face. "You know, I've spent most of my working life in art galleries, with other restorers, with the gallery directors and their administrators. It was a long time ago, 1911, I think. But what happened back then was not just known to them all, it was etched in their minds as an example, perhaps the prime example, of how a museum as famous as the Louvre could get it so wrong that it lost the *Mona Lisa*, Leonardo's masterpiece, *Ui Giaconda*, the most valuable painting in the world."

"How could it have happened?"

"You might ask. One Sunday evening as the Louvre was closing, a certain Vincenzo Peruggia who worked there as a technician hid in a broom cupboard while the museum emptied. When the time was right, he took down the *Mona Lisa* from its hanging, removed the frame, hid the painted wooden panel under his smock and walked out. Simple as that."

"I could be forgiven for saying it shouldn't have been possible."

"Worse, the theft wasn't even detected for two days. The museum was closed on Monday, the next day. When they saw the painting was missing they thought it had been removed for photography. Only the day after, when they realised what had happened, were the police called in. Peruggia was interviewed but he convinced them he was working elsewhere when the theft took place. All the time the masterpiece was hidden under his bed. The painting didn't come to light again for over two years."

Miles had been listening carefully. "It's a great story, Julia. But I'm struggling to get the relevance."

Julia smiled. "It's not the theft. It's what happened around the theft. Or at least what's supposed to have happened. What Peruggia did is rock solid fact. A matter of record. The truth came out when Peruggia tried to sell the painting through an art dealer in Florence. The dealer went to the authorities. When Peruggia was arrested he claimed all along he'd been motivated by pride for his country and was doing no more than returning the da Vinci masterpiece to its rightful place in Italy. He got two months and emerged as a hero. Meanwhile, the Italian authorities sent the painting on a tour of the country for the people to see it before returning it to the Louvre."

"OK, but I still don't get the connection."

"What's never been proven is the real reason why Peruggia stole the painting. The claim he did it for the sake of Italy was justification after the event, that much was plain for all to see. There had to be someone a whole lot brighter than Peruggia behind the theft."

"And there's evidence for that?"

"Nothing as clear as the case against Peruggia. The only evidence we have is a claim made in a newspaper article published in the nineteen thirties that the whole thing was a clever swindle."

"Let's say we go with it."

"The article claimed the mastermind was an Argentinian calling himself Eduardo di Valfierno. He pulled off the perfect crime, made millions from the theft and was never caught. That was because once the *Mona Lisa* had been stolen, he had no further interest in what happened to it. Long before the theft, he'd commissioned a French art forger to paint six identical copies. Di Valfierno then smuggled each of the copies into a different country, worldwide, his idea being that before the painting was stolen they wouldn't be noticed. When the publicity about the theft erupted, each of the wealthy men that di Valfierno had targeted in each of those countries was told they were being offered the original. Millions changed hands."

Miles was still sceptical. "But you don't know if the di Valfierno story is true?"

"Agreed. But don't you see, Miles? It doesn't matter if it's true or not. It's the perfect blueprint for a crime. Alessa Lando only has to know about it to be able to use it."

"A copy-cat crime."

"Yes. I think it went like this. Just like di Valfierno, Alessa Lando had multiple copies of a painting made by Westland. Only it wasn't the *Mona Lisa*, it was Picasso's *Weeping Woman*. She sold them through Pugot as if they were the real thing after Bellard had stolen the original. Pugot covered his tracks by working under a false name while he sold the paintings. One remained unsold. Perhaps Alessa Lando was too vain to destroy it. Perhaps, in recognition of Westland's talent and as a lover of art she couldn't bring herself to burn it. It doesn't matter. The copy survived and that's the one I saw in Lucca."

"And the scam was thirty years ago?"

"Yes. Alessa Lando pulled off the *Mona Lisa* swindle, I'm sure of it. No one knew where she got the money giving her the entree into the Lando dynasty. Now it's clear where she got it. And that's how Westland, Bellard and Pugot were involved. And it's why Pugot needed to place a letter with his solicitor as a way of preventing Alessa Lando from cleaning up the loose ends."

They'd made their way along Oxford Street and the traffic picked up speed as they headed towards the West End on the route that would take them back to the hotel.

Chapter 37

In a hire-by-the-day business office in downtown Austin, Agent Nate Craven explained what he wanted. "Just be here, as yourself, as James Blake."

"That's it?"

"Couldn't be more simple, James."

"So you are using me as bait."

He shook his head. "We wouldn't put it that way."

"How would you put it?"

He leaned back and took a deep breath. "OK. We've discussed this as a team. Is the operation going to be more successful if you know why you're here? I was against it, but my colleagues are convinced there's a better chance of success if you know."

"And?"

"We have a high profile family in our care and they require maximum protection."

"What kind of family?"

"You don't get to know that."

I guessed. "Politics."

Craven nodded. "But that's all you need to know. It's important to us because of that. And, so, it's important to you. You get me?"

"OK."

"We're giving them protection, twenty-four seven. But we've been asked to do more. To be more proactive. To protect the family by neutralising the threat against them."

"And that's where the bait comes in?"

He shook his head again. "I wish you wouldn't keep talking like that. We have intelligence there's an operative out there targeting the family but we don't know who it is. We do know he's connected to the Landos and we suspect he's also linked to the threats being made to you and your family."

I thought back to the images from Sollicciano Prison and Matteo Lando's threats against Julia and myself. "And that's connected with Agent Franks and what you got from the bugged Skype call."

"You're getting there."

"And I'm here to draw the operative out?"

He lowered his voice and tried to sound supportive. "Look, James. You'll be in danger. I won't try to hide it from you. But, think about it. You're already in danger. Your wife, your child, they're already in danger. Get closure on this and we end the whole thing once and for all. You won't have to be on the run from Matteo Lando or anyone else. We'll keep our family protected. And your family will be safe. You stand to gain as much as we do."

"What I don't understand is why do you need me? Why don't you move the family you're protecting? Move them someplace else?" Craven shrugged. "That's more stuff you don't need to know."

"Try me."

He sounded weary. "OK, if it helps, here it is. The people we're up against have intelligence from somewhere. There's a traitor from within our own organisation, maybe from within my own group. We don't know where. They know enough of what we're planning to mean they're only ever one step behind us. We've moved the family once, from California to here in Austin. But we're more than sure they know that. And that they'll be sending someone here. So, what do we do? Keep moving the family on? Hold them somewhere so secure they can't live their lives? No, we're drawing a line in the sand. We're making sure the family is in a well-protected, unassailable location here in Austin and we draw the assailant into a trap."

"We're back to me being the meat in the sandwich."

"I told you before, James. Please don't talk like that. You're the available option. The family is inaccessible. You're here. Low hanging fruit. And we'll be waiting. We'll get our man. Everyone can go back to living a normal life. You and your wife included."

"So, if you were going to take the trouble to convince me, why this? Why the rendition?"

"Who called it that? It's an arrangement about a matter of speed. Speed in getting you in place and making sure that when we put our proposition to you, you're where it makes sense – not in a few hours or days but right now. We do still have your full attention?"

I nodded. I didn't like the idea of being used by Craven and I didn't know if I could trust anything he was saying but he wasn't offering me much choice. He'd shown he could break any or all of the rules of law as he wished by bringing me here and taking me to Walls Unit in Huntsville. No one should be able to do that, but he'd just done it and would do more if I didn't co-operate.

He'd threatened the two people that meant the most to me in the world, three, if you counted my son. If I didn't go along with them Julia would not be protected in London or, worse, there was the insinuation that Craven might decide on some more direct assault on her. If I didn't play ball, Miles would be banged up in Walls Unit for thirty years.

No, I couldn't trust Craven but I knew I had to pretend I did and be convincing enough about it for him to believe I was in this for real.

It was the only way I could buy time to seek some way out.

I knew if I was going to convince him that I was now co-operating with him, I had work to do. I should have questions about what he wanted.

"OK. So, why are we saying I'm here?"

He looked up. "You have a cover story. And a cover story for that in case you need it. You're here as Charles Harrington and you're a rep for a company producing digital displays. You're in town to attend the Comicom trade fair here this week. That's what you tell the hotel staff. We believe you'll be credible in this role, given your background as a radio producer."

I shouldn't have been surprised Craven knew this about me but what he said still jarred. "OK, I can work with that. A nice touch to use Harrington. If they've been doing their homework, they may have connected me to the name. So, why am I really here?"

"As James Blake you've got hold of information about the family that's being targeted."

"And why would that matter to me?"

"Because you think they must have information to help you discover what the Landos have planned for you. This is a way you can protect your wife and child."

"And why would the family have that information?"

"They don't. It's enough you think they do."

"And why would I think that?"

"Because brother Miles told you and you can trust your brother."

"How will the operative know I'm here?"

"You can leave that to us." He sat back. "Remember, you have no public contact with the FBI. You're on your own as far as anyone from the outside is concerned."

"But you'll be watching?"

"Be assured, we'll be watching your every move. Even while you sleep."

"So you can be sure of my well being."

"So we can be sure you keep to your end of the deal. No contact with anyone unless it's part of the plan. And no contact with your wife or brother. If you do, the deal is off. You understand? The deal goes down. And if the deal goes down?"

"I know. You'll go straight for Miles and bang him up in Huntsville."

Craven smiled. "Good to hear we understand each other."

"Except for one thing. Cruel and inhuman treatment."

"Sounds like human rights. I thought we understood we were beyond that here."

I couldn't let this pass, not if there was a way of letting Julia know I was alive. "Cruel and inhuman treatment of my wife, Julia. Think about it. She has no idea where I am. As far as she knows I fell off the planet when you picked me up on the way to Charing Cross. Think how she's feeling. What harm would it do to give her just one call?"

Craven took his time. "I knew you'd ask that. Cruel and inhuman, huh? I guess no-one wants that on their headstone."

"And?"

"I don't like it, but I'll help you out. We followed you to your hotel in London before we picked you off the street. So we know where your wife is. She's under our surveillance and protection, just like I told you. She's safe and you have nothing to worry about on that score. I'll send an instruction for one of the team there to let your wife know you're safe and you're with us. And then you stick to the plan. You got that?"

"I've got it."

I didn't believe him but it was important he thought I did.

Nothing had changed what I was aching for – to let Julia know I was alive and to hear that she was safe.

Chapter 38

Back at the hotel, Miles updated Julia on progress with her request for a passport. "I made some calls while you were visiting Peggy Westland. I should have something by this evening. A guy in Wapping is on the case. His work is the best anybody's seen."

Julia thanked him. "That should keep the hotel manager happy, though he seems to have gone quiet about it. Maybe that's a good sign."

"Best to get him the ID to be sure."

Miles' phone rang. It was Adam Weston. "Do you have anything yet?"

Weston's voice was hard to pick out against a swell of background conversation. "I'm on a public phone, you don't need to know where. I'm getting more convinced they're on to me."

"Who's on to you?"

"Who else? The FBI. I'm spending too much time in there trying to find a way past their encryption. I'm sure they know it's me. It's only a matter of time before they trace me all the way back to the apartment."

"That's why you're calling?"

"No, it's to tell you not to come to the apartment again. It was a risk you came. It was foolish once we knew about the connection with politics. Can't you see the risk is too great? If I get anything I'll phone you like this or we'll meet somewhere else."

Miles was aware he needed to calm Weston. "Anything you want, Adam. I appreciate all you're doing to help, believe me. And I understand the risks you're taking. The information on Pugot was helpful. We think we're getting somewhere. We have another lead. H. Van De Baere, Ghent. They're a law firm."

"And?"

"I need information on a recent transaction."

Miles told Weston about the letter commissioned by Marcel Pugot that Julia had seen in Peggy Westland's apartment. "The original request for the letter goes back over thirty years."

Weston was not encouraging. "That's going to be off limits. Everything back then would be on paper."

"But a recent transaction?"

"We could be in luck. What do you need?"

"The names of the people who received Pugot's letter and any background research De Baere did to find them after those thirty years had passed."

"OK. I'll check it out and get back to you."

Weston ended the call.

Miles looked across to Julia. "He'll do his best."

Julia was grateful but disappointed. "This is all taking too long. James is still missing and there's still so much we don't know."

"Weston is not about to let us down. Trust me."

Julia knew this was something she would never be able to do. "Makes me feel so helpless."

Miles agreed. "I understand. Remember, James is my brother."

An hour later, Miles' phone rang again. It was Weston. Miles replied, "I thought you'd need longer."

The background chatter was the same but Weston was more upbeat. "Good news. Van De Baere is a go-ahead concern. They're scanning all their paperwork and archiving to hard drive. Their firewall is primitive."

"How far back do they go?"

"Just three years, so far."

"So, nothing on the original Pugot request?"

"No. But there's plenty on the recent stuff you asked for. The research they had to do to trace the families – it's all there. Enough of it to make you think that lawyers earn their fees."

"You had no trouble getting into their database?"

"Let's say it was easy compared with what the FBI serves up."

"What do you have?"

"Too much to tell. Let's meet for coffee in twenty minutes. Usual place."

Weston hung up.

Miles knew where the meeting would be – the cafe on the top floor of the Tate Modern. They'd used the location enough times before.

He looked up at Julia. "Weston has information from Ghent. I have to go to meet him so he can hand it over."

Chapter 39

Wolfgang Heller had little respect for the man he was now meeting. He was the one who had brought him to the unbearable heat of this place with its unbearable people. Yet Giuseppe Mordini was one of Alessa Lando's most trusted lieutenants. He'd served and protected her for over twenty years and carried his ugly and excessive body weight as a badge of honour.

To Heller he was a criminal of the old type, obvious and lacking in intelligence, unlike himself. Mordini might have a role as a fat man scaring shopkeepers into giving up their protection money but he was a liability in this modern world, a world in which he, Heller, was comfortable. Yet if Matteo said he should work with a man like Giuseppe Mordini he had to find a way for that to happen.

The meeting took place in Heller's hotel. The move to *Assura Suites*, ten-minutes from 6th Street, had been straightforward. His backup ID had not been questioned.

Giuseppe insisted on smoking even though the suite was designated as non-smoking. Heller had to struggle to control the impulse to rip the cigarette from the Italian's mouth. "You bring me here in this heat. You make me wait over twenty-four hours. I trust you have positive news?"

Giuseppe showed no sign of apology. "These things take time, Herr Heller. No doubt you have been occupying yourself. But be assured, I have the information."

The feeling was mutual. Like Heller, Giuseppe was here in the German's room only because Alessa wanted it. He hated the German. He loathed his insistence on propriety. He'd chosen to smoke to observe how the German responded when his patience was tried. This was useful information if, when the time came, he was asked to deal with the man. Understand your enemy's weaknesses, that's what Giuseppe had learned in his years with the Landos.

Heller was impatient. "So, tell me where they are."

Giuseppe paused, making his man wait. "The Ravitz family was taken to a gated compound up on Town Lake."

"With what security?"

"After they were scared out of San Diego, you won't be amazed to hear that it's at maximum. There are armed on-site police on twenty-four hour duty, patrolling and monitoring the complex. With what you'd expect. Security cameras, dogs, intruder alarms."

"And the Ravitz family?"

"They're in the most secure part at the rear of the compound. It's possible they have additional men assigned there just to them."

"You're making the location sound impregnable."

"I would say it is."

"So, why have you brought me here?"

"To deliver. You need to find a way to get in or to get them to leave the compound. We'd heard you're good at that kind of thing."

Heller hated how the Italian said "we". How he used that to point out how close he was to Alessa. "Anything else I need to know?"

Giuseppe told him the address. "There is something else."

"And that is?"

"Blake. James Blake is in Austin."

Heller was cautious about anything additional to the business at hand. In his experience, it introduced an unwelcome unpredictability. But this was the last thing he expected and, as a result, it concerned him all the more. "In Austin. Right now?"

"He's staying in a hotel right here in town."

"Where do we know this from?"

"It's come via Matteo, out of Sollicciano. There's no information more hard-earned than that."

"Do we know where Matteo got the information?"

Giuseppe shook his head. "No. But we know Blake is here under a false name – Charles Harrington. He must think he's safe to be here, traveling under a false identity, passing himself off as a techno attending the big computing convention, mixing with the crowd."

"And why do we think he's here in fact?"

"Same as you. He wants to find a way to get to the Ravitz family. He thinks they can lead him to us."

Chapter 40

The view over the Thames from the top floor cafe of the Tate Modern was one of the best in London.

Miles sat on one of the tall stools facing the long window, looking down on the Millennium Bridge and across the turbulent waterway to the dome of St Paul's.

It was unlike Adam Weston to be late. Miles had met him there many times before and it made sense to meet there again now that Weston had ruled out returning to the apartment.

Miles' thoughts turned to Julia and what he had to do to win back her trust, the question he'd been unable to face on Oxford Street. The answer was clear. He had to succeed in helping her find James. That would be the only thing to make it possible for her to forgive him. Right now, what Adam Weston had discovered from De Baere was their only lead and Weston was over an hour late. Miles could only hope that nothing had happened to him.

He was dragged out of his reverie as Adam Weston arrived and took the stool next to him. Weston's breathing was short. He must have been running. "Couldn't use the elevator. Had to take the stairs."

"Hold on." Miles tried to calm him. "What's got to you?"

"There are two of them. They were there as I was about to get into the elevator. They're FBI and they're on my case for sure. I knew I'd spent too much time in their database."

"Try to relax. How do you know it's them?"

"You think it's paranoia. It's not. Believe me, I'm sure it's them."

Miles decided it was easiest to agree. "OK. Let's say it is them. Where are they now?"

"I think I lost them. I took the stairs to the second floor and used my card to get into the Klein exhibition. They'd need a ticket to get in and the ticket office is way back on the ground floor. They wouldn't want to blow their cover and make a scene with the exhibition attendant. I went in and left straight away by the exit near the exhibition shop. Then I took the stairs up here."

Weston took a USB stick from his pocket. "It's all here. The names of those sent the Pugot letter. And the background search information that De Baere carried out to find them."

"That's great." Miles took the stick and handed back an envelope. "Your fee, as we agreed."

Weston took the money. He put it in his jacket pocket without checking the amount. "I'm out of here."

Miles turned to look at him for the first time. "Stay safe."

"I will. Don't stay here."

Weston made his way out of the building. Looking down on the open pathway between the Millennium Bridge and the museum entrance, Miles had a bird's eye view of the diminutive figure of Weston as he hurried away towards the *Founders Arms* and *The Doggett*.

Miles checked to make sure the USB stick was safe in his trousers pocket. He was shaken to realise that Weston could have been right about being followed.

He headed for the stairs and made his way out of the museum, trying to make it look as if he was part of a large group of French tourists who were completing their visit.

Paranoia is contagious, he knew that, but Weston was a convincing portrayal of a man under surveillance.

Miles made it to the newspaper office in The Strand that he worked from when he was in London. He didn't think he'd been followed but there was no way of being sure.

The USB stick loaded into his desktop computer without difficulty. He opened it and looked over the files that Weston had copied to it from his hacking of the De Baere records. Weston had done well. There were hundreds of files, too many to look through here in the office.

Miles opened each of the files and selected 'print'. The information began spilling out on the office printer they all shared.

His desk mate, Angus Wilson, looked up from his work. "A little homework?"

Miles stood over the printer, making sure no one would collect the pages by mistake or see the volume of material he was printing. He called back, "Something to keep me busy for a while. You know, a journalist's job."

"Is never done."

"Something like that."

When the printing was finished he had over three hundred pages. Miles placed them in a document box file and returned to his desk.

Yes, Weston had done well. It would take some time to discover just what he'd found.

Chapter 41

It had been too long since Miles had left to meet Weston. Julia was unsettled to find she was concerned for him. She tried to tell herself it was because she needed information that might lead her to James and it was the absence of news about James she was anxious about. Yet when she opened the hotel room door to let Miles in she had to stop herself telling him she'd been concerned for his safety. "That took a long time."

Miles sat down and faced her. "Problems with Adam Weston."

"He didn't show?"

"No, he was there, late and wired. He handed me the De Baere material. He's sure he's being followed."

"And that's getting to you? You look stressed."

"The way Weston was would get to anyone. He's convinced the FBI are on his case."

"Why would they connect to Weston?"

"He's sure he's overstayed his hacker's welcome and they've tracked him from that."

"Do you think they've made the connection from him to us?"

"He doesn't know you're here, so even if they try they're not going to find you from Weston."

Julia was relieved. "What was he able to give you?"

Miles opened the document box file. "I printed it out from the information Weston took from the De Baere database."

Julia was disconcerted by the volume of material. Weston had done well. He'd found the correspondence between the partners and their assistants in the De Baere firm as they worked to fulfil Pugot's request that the letter he'd penned all those years before should be sent to each of those who had been duped into buying a copy of Picasso's *Weeping Woman*. Pugot's instructions had been precise. If the original purchaser was no longer alive, the letter should be sent to their descendants. What they had here were the emails and attachments that told the story of how De Baere had investigated to find details of the correct recipients of each letter.

Miles could see she was pleased with the amount of material Weston had delivered. "Weston is good. Once he gets in past their firewall there's little to stop him downloading anything and everything. That's one of our problems. There's so much material here, it's going to take time to go through it all."

There was information on five families. Julia saw straight away that one could be eliminated.

"McKenzie. Alex McKenzie. Named by Pugot as one of the purchasers of a fake Picasso. Died in 2001. A loner. Didn't marry. No heirs. Gave his fortune to charity on his death. De Baere decided no letter should be sent."

Miles nodded. "Agreed. We shouldn't include him."

"That leaves four families. Two each."

They agreed to share out the pages.

Miles smiled. "Quicker this way."

"I'll take Ravitz and Montgomery. You take Walsh and Davidson."

Miles took his share of the pages. "All four are in the US. I don't know if it's a good or a bad thing."

As she read through her share of the documents, it didn't take Julia long to understand that progress was going to be slow.

She paused and turned to Miles. "De Baere were thorough."

Miles looked up. "Maybe you'd be thorough if you knew you were going to be paid for each piece of information you found."

"There's so much here, yet nothing that leads directly to any of the families. We have postal addresses for each. Mine are from San Diego and Boston."

"And mine are from New York and Albuquerque."

"If your addresses are like mine they're not residences."

Miles nodded. "Like so many people with wealth they have holding addresses at banks or post office bureau. Then the mail is forwarded. There's no guarantee the recipients even live in the same town as that in the holding address."

"And the rest of the paperwork will take days to go through. Meanwhile, James is missing and we have no idea where he is."

"What else do we know?"

Julia tried to be clear. "We have what Franks said when he called in Weymouth. He said he wanted James to help. Jim accused him of wanting to use us as bait in some kind of trap to uncover a threat to an important US family."

"And we have what Adam Weston found when he hacked the FBI database. The case Franks was working on was classified and concerned with politics. So which of the four families would fit that bill?"

They began using Miles' laptop to search for political connections. They found that Montgomery was out. The family business was in manufacture of farm machinery. It was a good way to get rich but nothing in the public record suggested any political involvement greater than lobbying and special interest pleading.

It was a different matter with the Ravitz family. When she saw the details on the screen, Julia shouted out, "That could be them! Eli Ravitz has died but his son, Elmore Ravitz, is a candidate for Senator who's tipped to one day run for the Presidency. He's based in San Diego. We may be able to find him from the delivery address."

Miles tried not to look discouraging. "Hold on, Julia. I'm checking the other families. Both have political connections. Stephen B Davidson's father-in-law is a one-time Mayor of Albuquerque and the Walsh family go way back in New York Irish politics. It could be any one of those three families that we're looking for."

Julia lay back in her chair and focused on not giving in to the helplessness that was about to overtake her. There was a way, a way back to James. She whispered that to herself over and over.

She had to think, and think straight.

She knew what had set in place the damaging train of events that threatened her family. Pugot's death had triggered the release of the letters to those duped into handing over good money for a fake painting. She'd seen Picasso's *Weeping Woman* in Lucca and as a result she was a threat to the Landos, if only that she might one day give evidence against them in court, and she knew enough of the ruthlessness of the Landos to know they would seek to remove all loose ends so that threats to them as yet unknown could not arise. She was one of those loose ends but knowing this had taken her no further to discovering what had happened to James, who had him and where they'd taken him. Now the recovery of the De Baere documents was threatening to end the same way.

Her thoughts turned back to Miles.

Why hadn't he told her more about his investigation of the Landos?

Another of their long silences had descended. Julia could sense the unease between them whenever the conversation stopped, as if he was all the time waiting for her to question or even accuse him.

"Tell me more about your investigation?"

"The Landos?"

Julia nodded.

Miles began, "I thought I'd told you."

"You haven't said anything much."

"I wanted to finish the Lando story. Finish the family. I've made progress. You know, I'm on to them again. They're shipping more cocaine than they ever did when Alfieri was alive and, if I'm right, they're using the same supply channels. I'm close, Julia. Close to blowing their operation wide open."

"Even though Matteo has been sent down for life?"

"That's no barrier for him. He's head of the family now and he has no problem operating from Sollicciano prison."

Nothing had changed. Miles was always chasing the next story. This was the official line that he might have told an editor when asked to explain what he was doing. This was getting her nowhere closer to finding James.

She raised her voice. "Miles, why can't you tell me what's really happening in the investigation?"

Miles looked away. "I don't know what you mean."

"You can tell me. Trust me."

He hesitated and then, drawing courage, he spoke again. "You're right. I'm not being straight with you but there are reasons why I haven't been able to tell you. I wasn't sure myself that I hadn't dragged you and Jim into all this again. After Florence, I knew you'd never be able to forgive me but I couldn't bear the thought that I'd endangered you both again. I couldn't face up to it if it was true. You understand?"

She nodded. "But we know now that as soon as I'd seen the Picasso, this was bound to happen one day, sooner or later. You don't have anything to feel guilty about what's happening now."

Miles looked Julia in the eye for the first time in a long time. "I'm glad to hear it. At least I'm half-forgiven."

She reached forward and took his hand. "Miles, I was debased by Alfieri Lando. I can never forgive him for what he did to me. Nor what he and his family did to Emelia. The corruption he brought to everything he touched. And I didn't think I'd ever be able to forgive you for bringing that evil into my life. But I mean it. I forgive you. You couldn't have known such a terrible thing could happen in Florence. You can't spend the rest of your life atoning for that mistake. I do forgive you."

Tears formed in Miles' eyes and ran down his cheeks. He whispered, "Thank you."

Julia felt relieved that she'd made her peace with him. It was part of the healing process that she found as difficult as any other yet she realised now how important it was.

Yet, this moment of reconciliation should not delay them. Time was running out in finding James. It didn't help to see Miles in tears like this. Hard though it was, she had to move the conversation on.

"You said there was another reason."

Miles wiped away the tears with the back of his hand. "I didn't want to give false hope. The investigation in the States hasn't been going well. It's confused and confusing. I get the feeling that despite all I know about investigative journalism, I'm in danger of being out of my depth. I didn't want to involve you with all my problems when you have enough of your own."

"What's the problem?"

He tried to smile. "Just that I think I'm going to get hauled in before I get even close to breaking the story." He paused. "And the fact that the main contact, the one who's on the inside feeding me information, might be unreliable."

Julia could feel depression returning. "We don't have anything. James has been missing for over thirty-six hours and we have no way of finding him."

"There is one thing. I don't want you to get your hopes up. It's likely to be a dead end. It's something that's come into play now you've told me about the Picasso."

Julia held his hand tighter. "What is it?"

"It's something I'd discounted. As I told you, in my business you learn to concentrate on the story in hand and dismiss anything that might be a diversion from the main goal."

"Like you dismissed what Bellard had to say?"

"Yes, like I put that on the back burner." Miles cleared his throat. "Well, there's a contact I've been working with in Mexico, trying to get information about the drugs supply route used by the Landos. Someone who was helpful at first but who's been less helpful of late. I'm not sure if he's been trying to play me to lead me into the hands of the FBI or even if he's an FBI agent himself who's undercover in Mexico. Or if he has another agenda all his own. I have no way of being sure. He's not been giving me the information I need and I've been avoiding him."

"So why could he be of help now?"

"Well, strange as it seemed to me at the time, he's been pumping me for information on what happened in Florence. About the Lando interest in art. I couldn't see how that was anything other than a diversion at best and something more sinister at worst. But after what you've told me, I'm not so certain."

Julia released Miles' hand and sat back. "Why would he be interested in what happened in Florence?"

"I've told him nothing. I didn't want to implicate you any further."

"That doesn't matter. I don't know why, Miles, but I sense this is important. It's the art swindle that got James and me involved in this again, I'm sure of it. What's the name of your contact?"

"Luiz Reyas."

"Can you reach him?"

"He's been messaging me every day. I just have to reply."

Julia smiled.

Miles left to arrange to make the contact.

Julia ordered room service. When the waiter arrived, he was accompanied by the hotel manager who made a great show of demanding to see Julia's passport.

"The forty-eight hours are up, madam. I need proof of identity."

She tried to sound as unapologetic as possible. "My husband has been delayed a further twenty-four hours. It was unavoidable."

The manager took his time in agreeing. "All right. Twenty-four hours more but not a moment longer."

Chapter 42

Perhaps it was her age but these days Alessa Lando found herself thinking more often about her family and its past.

The story of how her grandfather, Esteban Lobos Ventura, had gone to Europe and returned home to Buenos Aires with a fortune was one she would have liked to share with the world – how he'd pulled off the perfect crime, right under the noses of those who thought they were much more cultured and sophisticated than him.

It was a stroke of genius to find Vincenzo Peruggia, an undervalued technician at the Louvre, and to convince him he should steal *Ui Giaconda* for the sake of Italy. Nothing was more certain to succeed than the actions of a patriot, one serving a higher cause with a determination denied to those who acted for money alone. Yet, money had been required.

Grandfather Esteban had gambled everything on this single chance. Before leaving Argentina, he'd sold the family home for less than it was worth to have the cash available now, when he needed it – money he used to bribe Peruggia to carry out the theft. Even the patriot must eat, Peruggia had told Esteban. And he needed money for the forger.

Finding Michel Patron couldn't have been easy; someone who would not blink at being asked to produce not one but six copies of the *Mona Lisa;* someone good enough to make those copies so exact and so much like they were painted over four hundred years ago that even an expert might be fooled.

Of course, when Patron was approached, he wasn't told that the real *Mona Lisa* was going to be stolen. Here was this South American with money to burn who had somehow learned of the reputation of the greatest forger of his day and wanted to buy not one but six copies of the masterpiece. Who was Patron to ask why? And if the South American was using what anyone could see was a false identity, what did it matter? It was none of Patron's business. The payment was good and was in cash. Money was scarce in Paris in 1911 with war on the way.

Yes, thought Alessa, this had been the second brilliance of Esteban's plan – to engage Patron three months ahead of the theft, to give him no indication of the real purpose of having the copies made, to allow time for the ageing process that Patron applied to his work to take hold so the copies would look old. Time to smuggle the copies into the chosen countries around the world before the theft took place when no one would be looking for the painting.

The further brilliance was to not let Peruggia know the full extent of the plan. Since it had cost so much to have it stolen, he'd expected Esteban to come to him within a week to collect the *Mona Lisa.* Esteban gambled that when he did not make contact Peruggia would assume something had gone wrong and Esteban had been forced to flee. He gambled that Peruggia would take this as a further sign that his gods were on his side and he should keep the masterpiece hidden until the time came when he could sell it, knowing if it was found in his possession he would be able to defend himself with the claim that he'd acted for Italy, to restore his nation's pride. It was less of a gamble that the unexpected prospect of becoming a rich man would be enough to propel Peruggia on this course.

All Esteban wanted was for it to be known that the *Mona Lisa* had been stolen. The newspapers made sure of that. The story went round the world. He did not care that Peruggia was caught two years later when he tried to sell the painting to a Florence art dealer, nor that he was sent to trial in Italy, found guilty and released after serving just a few months. It did not matter that he emerged from prison as a hero of Italy for trying to return one of the nation's masterpieces to its rightful home, nor that in the fullness of time the *Mona Lisa* was returned to the Louvre, because in the years between the furore over the theft of the painting and its recovery, Esteban made his fortune.

The final brilliance of Esteban's plan was to recognise that rich and powerful men who made their money at the margins of legal society would be unable to resist the temptation of owning the most valuable painting in the world. Knowing it had been stolen would not deter them. As long as they had it and it was theirs to keep, to hold in secret, that would be enough. The fact that this would be a guilty secret to be revealed only to those they honoured with the knowledge of the secret made the thrill of owning the painting all the greater. Yes, Esteban had understood well the egoism of such men.

If the plan could work once, it could be made to work again. Whoever bought the painting wasn't going to tell the world what they had done. It was a perfect scam.

Esteban sold the first copy to a Mexican rancher who'd grown fat making illegal cattle imports from the Unites States. The second was sold to an Italian-origin landowner in Chile. The third went to a minor noble in the Romanov dynasty in Imperial Russia. The fourth to a US Senator who had made a quick killing selling armaments to Europe. The fifth to a member of the British landed gentry. The sixth had not been sold. How apt that this remained in the family.

Esteban sold each for one fifth of the market price. It was a bargain for each man, yet one fifth of priceless is a lot of money in any currency and in any age. Esteban got paid five times, not once. He became a wealthy man, returning to Buenos Aires with over one thousand times the money he'd raised in the sale of his home.

He didn't have to concern himself with the shock of realisation that came to each of the men who'd bought a *Mona Lisa*. It must have hit them like a sledgehammer once the news of the recovery of the real *Mona Lisa* and Peruggia's trial spread worldwide. He didn't have to concern himself with the consequences of the humiliation of those men that came with the knowledge that they'd been duped, nor the fact that those in whom they'd confided their guilty secret came to doubt their judgment and the tragic consequences that followed. Grandfather Esteban was by then living the comfortable and secure life of the rich man he'd become. And she, Alessa, had been an outcome.

It pleased her that the family had been guarded so well from the knowledge of how their fortune had arisen, how Esteban had even laid a false trail that the whole plan had been carried out by a mysterious Argentine called

Eduardo di Valfierno with a forger other than Patron, so that, if anyone began to investigate the theft of the *Mona Lisa* as the clever scam it was, they would be looking for a non-existent perpetrator.

Behind every great fortune lies a great crime. This had been true of each of the families that Esteban had chosen to purchase a copy of the *Mona Lisa*. Perhaps, on a small scale, it was his way of righting the wrongs at the same time as he made himself rich.

His crime had been special, one that showed his superiority over those he'd duped, for, if you discounted the consequences of their bruised egos, his was a victimless crime. If there were those who might claim the status of victim, it was clear they deserved what they got.

Alessa came out of her thoughts. Yes, it had been a superior crime and one that had served her family well. But their wealth was used up by the time she came of age. Back in 1983, it had been up to her to find a way of restoring the family's fortune.

Esteban had been just thirty years old when he'd made the family rich. She was also just thirty back then, when she'd found a way to gather together the means to act.

Chapter 43

Before recent events, Elmore Ravitz was preparing for a good year.

The efforts he'd made to become electable were about to pay off. The charity fund raisers, the celebrity dinners, the work with the Party, the image consultant sessions, were all about to prove worthwhile as he gained the nomination for Senator and then saw the opinion polls give him a ten point lead over his rival.

Then the letter arrived.

It would have been easy to ignore it, to let it pass in favour of the realisation that nothing should stand in the way of the Senate seat. That would have been too easy and, in any case, wouldn't have been possible, he knew that.

He'd never tried explaining the whole story to his wife, Leah, but the time had now come.

Nothing was ideal here on Town Lake but at least they were safe from harm and they had a degree of privacy – when the FBI men posted to protect them would leave them in peace.

Daughter Jenny was asleep. The guards had made their latest round of security checks and he was alone with Leah. It was time to tell her.

"Honey, I want to be completely straight with you. If I'm going to make it all the way, you can't be placed in a situation where anything will come as unwelcome news to you, especially as First Lady."

There, he'd said it. In eight or twelve years' time he would be a viable candidate for President. Influential members of the Party were talking in those terms. A campaign to raise the funding he would need was well underway.

Leah knew something like this was coming. She'd not seen him look this troubled; those signs of inner turmoil couldn't be hidden, not from her. In the twenty years they'd been together she'd learned to read his moods, to understand his inner life. Everything she knew now told her this was bad. "Tell me, honey. There's more to why we have to move here, isn't there?"

He held her hand. "I want to tell you everything, right from the start. I want you to know everything and that's not going to be easy. I don't want you to think the worst of me."

"You know I'd never do that."

"It's about my father, Eli. He had enemies. In truth, he never had many real friends, just a bunch of acquaintances held together by the respect they had for him."

"How do you mean, respect? Makes him seem, well, somehow shady."

"That's what I have to tell you. There's no good way to hedge around it. He was a criminal. The money in this family came from drugs."

There, he'd said that too.

"I thought it was from an import/export business."

"It was. Only there wasn't much export, I have to tell you. He brought drugs in from Mexico. Just until he made enough to go legitimate and establish the family, send me to a good school, give me a college education, put me where I am today. None of that was easy – not when you're dealing with Mexico's and San Diego's finest."

Leah was shocked but tried not to show it. "That was the past. This is now. Those days are behind you. Behind us. You have a great future. What makes you want to dwell on the past at a time like this?"

"I wish it was that simple. Truth is, the past began to catch up with us once the letter arrived."

"Letter?"

Elmore went to the study desk, opened it and removed an envelope containing a single sheet of paper.

He gave the letter to Leah. She read it, taking in every word. "It's from a lawyer in Belgium and it's addressed to your father. I don't understand. What has this got to do with what's happening to us now? It's not about what you were saying about drugs, is it?"

"Not directly, my dear, but that's where this leads."

He told her how his father had been one of those fooled into buying a worthless copy of a stolen painting, Picasso's *Weeping Woman*, believing it to be the original.

"I guess the letter came here because Eli's no longer with us and the lawyer who sent it was under instruction to mail it to the next of kin."

"This man Pugot who asked for the letter to be sent, he was the art dealer?"

Ravitz nodded.

"Your father bought the picture knowing it was stolen?"

"That didn't matter to him. Such precious things were owned by those who didn't deserve them. He'd made it to the top the hard way. Why shouldn't he have the best if it pleased him? But when it emerged that the painting was a fake, he was angry. He was a vengeful man. Yet he couldn't find the identity of those who had swindled him. He marked it down as unfinished business and that's the way it stayed."

"Until now."

"Yes, until I received the letter."

Leah was still struggling to understand the significance of the letter. "So what does the letter change? Why can't it stay as unfinished business?"

Ravitz leaned forward. "That's just the point, my dear. You see, we now know the name of the person who swindled my father. It was Alessa Lando. She took the money from my father and, not content with that, she used it to finance the entry of her family into the drugs business in Mexico. They should have had more sense than to do that with someone they'd used in an art swindle but we now know that's just what they did."

"And that puts us in danger?"

"It does. It's certain Eli wasn't the only one to be taken in by the Landos. People like that are greedy. They worked the swindle with more than one fake copy of the painting and that means there is more than one copy of the letter out there. Those people will start looking for answers. Those answers are going to lead to the connection between Eli and the Lando family. Between us and the Landos."

Leah was becoming more concerned. "And it could end your political career?"

Ravitz nodded. "There are no votes in you or your family having been involved in drugs. Once that connection was made my political career would be over for sure. You can see why I had to act on the letter. But I made a mistake. I went after her, Alessa Lando and her criminal gang."

"What are you saying?"

"They deserved no better. I had words with friends in the FBI. They sympathised with my problem. I didn't mention drugs. Just the art swindle. They were helpful."

"You're frightening me. Why was it a mistake?"

Elmore gave an unconvincing smile. "They tried to get to her, but she'd disappeared. No contact was made. But by then I'd already made my first mistake. When I sent the FBI after her, she was alerted. What had been kept secret all those years was now out in the open. The art dealer, Pugot, died, did I tell you that?"

Leah shook her head. "No, but it makes sense from the letter."

"In an accident, for Pete's sake. He must have threatened Alessa Lando all those years ago. He didn't trust her. If anything happened to him, he'd arrange for his lawyer to send out letters naming her to the families that had been swindled. That's why we got our letter when we did. Alessa Lando was alerted to Pugot's death and got to find out the letters had been sent naming her."

"Don't blame yourself. You don't know that she might have found this out anyway by other means."

"I guess that's right. But in any case, I'd done a good job of making sure she knew."

Leah was finding it hard to hold back the tears. "And that's the real reason why we had to leave San Diego?"

Ravitz squeezed her hand. "There's only one way people like the Landos know how to react. They attack first. They seek to eliminate the threat to them before anything can happen to them."

"So we're under direct threat?"

He nodded. "There's an operative out there. At least one, maybe a second. We're their target. It's why we're here, surrounded by security."

Leah shuddered. "And all set off by the letter?"

He nodded again.

"But we're safe here? We don't have to worry?"

"That's right, my dear. We're safe here."

"You said it was your first mistake."

He looked away. "When I contacted the FBI it wasn't a clean contact. There was confusion over names. I got through to the wrong part of the Agency. Not the part that's with us, if you know what I mean. The agent they put on the case wasn't someone we could trust to keep what he discovered away from the wider authorities. But it's been sorted out. Agent Craven is assigned to the case now. He's one of us. He's sorting this mess out."

Jenny Ravitz turned over in bed. Her parents had been quieter than usual but she'd heard enough to know the reason why they were here.

Chapter 44

When Miles replied to Luiz Reyas' last message, the reply that came back was simple: *Urgent. Meet in Austin, Texas. AM 22nd*.

Miles determined he could get there in time via Heathrow and Chicago O'Hare if he left within the hour.

He phoned Julia from the Newspaper to where he'd returned to plan the trip. "It's come. The message from Reyas. I need to meet him in Austin. Means I'll be gone at least three days."

Julia felt at a loss that she'd come to depend on this man who, a short while before, she'd done everything to avoid. "I can manage."

"I'm arranging protection for you. I can charge it through the Newspaper. Mark Craig. He's ex-police and experienced. When I briefed him he asked all the right questions."

"What did you tell him?"

"You're a witness to a crime I'm investigating and you may be in danger. Oh, and that you're pregnant."

"You didn't tell him about Franks and the Landos?"

"I thought I'd leave it to you to decide how much to tell him."

"And what do I tell the hotel manager?"

"Simple. Craig is your brother. He's come to keep you company while James is away on business. By the way, your passport is ready. Craig will collect it and bring it with him."

"Is Craig armed?"

"He shouldn't be. But he will be carrying. You can depend on him. He's got me out of more than one difficult situation. I trust him. You should too."

Julia didn't sound as relieved as Miles had hoped. "I'll do my best to convince the manager."

"Craig will take a room in the hotel like any other paying customer. He can help you handle the manager, I'm sure of that."

"Why Austin?"

"It's where Reyas wants to meet, that's all I know. I'll find out when I get there."

Julia spoke at a whisper. "Take care, Miles. Look after yourself."

Chapter 45

It was evening in Austin and I was playing my part in Craven's plan by sitting in the bar of the Warren Richardson Hotel trying not to be out of place even though I had the haunted look that comes from being drugged, shipped five thousand miles on a military aircraft and then kept under constant surveillance.

I was surrounded by the expected, well-heeled crowd who'd found their way into the air-conditioned bar to escape the August heat.

A blonde-haired woman in a business suit had come to sit next to me. "You look terrible."

I replied in my best British accent. "It's the jet lag. Always makes me feel bad."

She smiled. "And, don't tell me, you Brits don't take well to the Austin heat."

"We don't."

She'd drawn close enough now for me to smell her hundred-dollar-a-bottle perfume.

She whispered, "Don't overdo it, James. I work for the Firm. Just make it look like I'm picking you up. You can manage that, can't you? But don't get any ideas. I work for Craven and he wants you to know this is business, straight business. OK? Which is not to say I don't find jet-lagged Brits attractive."

"Just so I know?"

"Yeah. Just so you know."

"No, I mean, what's your name?"

"Call me Miller."

"Agent Miller?"

"Debbie Miller. Less of the agent."

"So this is what we do. We wait here."

She smiled. "You got it. And you get me a drink."

I called over the barman. Agent Miller knew what she wanted. "Single malt. Ice. No water."

The barman obliged.

It was a false existence if ever there was one – pretending to be here for the Comicom trade fair.

I complained to Agent Miller. "How long do we have to keep up this charade?"

She downed the whisky and held out her glass for another. "As long as it takes."

"And why here, in this bar?"

"It's the way Craven wants it. He's methodical. This is the place where he can get enough of the right personnel in position to bring the assailant down. Once he reveals himself."

I didn't like the sound of that. "With me as the come on."

She didn't answer. Instead she looked down at the empty glass. "Now you couldn't say the barman was busy, could you?"

I spent a nervous four hours in the hotel bar.

That did nothing for my paranoia.

While keeping up the small talk with Agent Miller, I was all the time positioning myself so I could look around the place without this showing.

I couldn't recognise any of Craven's team who'd been on the plane or with me at Huntsville. When I took another look around a little later, I could see that Craven had joined a group of three at the far end of the bar who exchanged banter in what looked like a good-natured night out with friends. I had to take it on trust they were Craven's men and that they were on duty. Yet it was clear the priority was not to protect me but, rather, to catch the assailant once I'd been targeted.

I found myself looking at every newcomer and asking myself the question – is this him, is this the operative these people were so determined to catch that they would lay my life on the line?

There was one man, a Mexican with whitened teeth and eyes all the time so wide open that the white below his eyelids showed. I was convinced he was the one – something about him said he no more belonged here than I did.

I whispered to Miller, "I think that's him. Standing at the bar. Near the centre. The Mexican."

Miller whispered back. "What makes you think that?"

"Just the way he looks."

She smiled. "If it was that easy, this whole operation would be a cake walk."

"You don't think it's him?"

She smiled again. "It's not him."

"How can you be sure?"

"We have word the one we're expecting is European."

I felt relieved. I looked over at the Mexican again. He looked like a normal business type once more. The paranoia was making anything or anyone look suspicious.

I returned my thoughts to Miller. "OK. It's not him. But sooner or later one of them is going to be the one you're looking for. Doesn't that make you think?"

"Think what, Charles?"

"Well, the way Craven has this thing set up doesn't leave much to doubt. The plan is not to protect me but to catch your man when he attacks. And you're not out there with Craven's men, you're up here with me in the line of fire. Doesn't that worry you?"

She gave me a condescending look. "You don't get it, do you? In my line of work this is what we do."

I wished I had Miller's courage.

The evening passed. I thought I had identified at least two others, European types this time, who fitted the bill but I was wrong again. In the event, the assailant did not show.

Craven summed it up. "Nothing tonight. But that doesn't mean the perp won't show."

I was escorted at a distance back to my room.

Chapter 46

Wolfgang Heller didn't like what he'd seen out at Town Lake.

And he liked even less the idea that the Englishman Blake was in Austin. Heller had been to the Warren Richardson Hotel and had seen him but hadn't stayed long enough to be observed.

Both were traps. The compound at Town Lake was so well defended that any reasonable person would have deduced that five like him would have found it impossible to make the hit.

He'd expected Elmore Ravitz to be well-defended. After all, he had power and influence and all those friends in high places. That influence had been used to threaten the well-being of Heller's good friend Matteo Lando and, for God's sake, his mother. Here was a man who hid behind the gloss of decency when all along, as Heller knew so well, he had no right to anything of the kind.

So, he was supposed to be drawn to the Englishman as the easier target. He wasn't about to fall for that. He knew they'd be waiting for him. How crude they'd been in this. As if he would oblige them. They had to be made to understand he was a more worthy opponent than that.

No, he would not do what was expected. Indeed, as he'd learned to his advantage more than once, this was the moment to do what was unexpected.

He took a taxi and visited the first travel agent he found. He booked a return flight to Albuquerque.

There were others on the list. A hit in Albuquerque when eyes were focused on Austin would produce consternation amongst those seeking to stop him. When he returned to Austin, the chances of making the hit would be greater.

He returned to the hotel and lay on the bed. He called up Wagner's *Parsifal* on his MP3 player. The small earphones were not adequate to do full justice to the magnificence of the music yet his mind cleared as he listened. The sense of order that was so lacking in the world out there was being restored with every note. This was a music for decent god-fearing people, an antidote to the trash he encountered all around him in this place and, more than that, a reminder of the true heroism that survived in men like him. Men unafraid to look truth in the face.

He let his mind drift. He saw himself picking up the lance, the spear that pierced Christ's side. He felt the superhuman power that holding the cherished object was giving him – the power he drew deep inside him in moments like this.

Luiz Reyas had followed Heller to the hotel and had noticed the brief interest he'd shown in the Englishman who waited in the lounge. He'd then followed Heller to the travel agent. The assistant there looked pleased when Reyas pushed a fifty-dollar bill across the counter. "The German. Where was he headed?"

The assistant took the bill. "Albuquerque. You want a ticket?"

Chapter 47

DI Reid knew he had to check it out. They could be hiding James in the posh apartment in Wilbraham Place that he'd seen the Blake woman visit. One million was good but two million was a world of difference if you wanted to feel comfortable amongst the rich.

He chose to leave it until after dark to make his way over to Blenheim Mansions. He checked for security cameras and could see none. That's what you get with established wealth. Who would want those ugly things destroying the fine appearance of the building?

There was no point in being subtle. The only way he was going to get into the Westland apartment was to use his CID card – but not as DI Reid. For circumstances like this he kept a fake card in another name, DI Billingham. The card he'd shown at the vehicle pound and at the Allegro Hotel. This was useful if you wanted to avoid being traced if you were forced to identify yourself after roughing up a suspect or for times like these when a full-on personation was required. Reid had not used it often but the money spent in having the fake card made had been repaid many times over.

He pressed the bell to apartment number 6. After a pause the intercom crackled and he announced himself. "Police. Inspector Billingham. I have some questions."

It was a good sign. The Westland woman replied and sounded anxious. "Can't this wait?"

"It's urgent. It's about Julia Blake."

That did the trick – the electric lock was slipped and he was inside.

He checked again for security cameras. You had to admire the confidence of these people. There were none to be seen.

The door to the apartment was opened as soon as he arrived. Peggy Westland was being cautious. "You don't mind if I see some identification?"

He showed her the Billingham card. "Mike Billingham. I just have a few questions."

She showed him in. "It must be urgent to come here at this late hour, Inspector."

He took the seat he was offered. "It is. I understand you know Julia Blake?"

"What's this in connection with?"

Reid decided on a straightforward approach. "Julia Blake. She's missing. So is her husband, James. This is a routine missing persons enquiry. We're checking anyone who might know them and I was told you're close to Mrs. Blake. Do you know where she is?"

Peggy Westland was a poor liar. "No, Inspector. I haven't seen her for, well, it must be several years now. Not since her return from Florence. You must understand I'm in mourning for my husband, Richard."

"Sorry to trouble you. Have you seen her husband, James?"

She was growing more confident she was in control. "I haven't seen either of them. Now, if there's nothing more,

Inspector, I have much to do and, since there's nothing I can say to help you, I'd like you to leave."

Reid could see she wasn't going to help him. He'd come this far, further than he'd ever been. If he was going to do this thing, if he was to become the wealthy man he knew he deserved to be, he had to go that short distance further. Blake could be hiding anywhere in this large apartment. He wouldn't forgive himself if his man was here and he let him go.

Reid stood, walked over and picked the Westland woman up. She was nine stone or less and it was easy to carry her to the bedroom using the fireman's lift they'd taught him in rescue and safety training. She was shouting and trying to kick but the fact he'd approached her without warning had overwhelmed her and her protests were not going to alert anyone.

In the bedroom he threw her on the bed and pushed a pillow over her face. She wasn't big but she was a fighter. He had to use all his strength to hold her down until the shaking of her legs stopped and he knew he'd killed her.

There, he'd done it. There was no way back now.

There wasn't much to connect him to the crime. There would be no CCTV to analyse. There was little light with no one around. It was unlikely he'd been seen entering or leaving the building. There would be no questions about DI Billingham because the only person who knew of his existence here apart from himself was lying lifeless beneath him. There was nothing to connect what had happened here with the DI who visited the Allegro and the vehicle pound.

Reid began the search. He took time to examine each of the rooms. He opened cupboards and peered inside. He looked under beds. He opened the shower cubicle door. Blake wasn't here.

He sat for some time in the lounge and tried to collect his thoughts. Why had the Westland woman lied to him? It would have been simple enough to state that Julia Blake had been here earlier that day. Peggy Westland was hiding something and if it wasn't James Blake it must be something else.

He began a more thorough search. He turned on the desktop computer. As expected, there was no password protection. He began searching the desktop looking for files but there was nothing out of the ordinary there. He looked in drawers, in kitchen cupboards and found nothing of interest there. One place remained, a place so obvious he was annoyed with himself for not having searched it up to now.

The antique desk was the centrepiece of the lounge. One of the drawers was locked but there was no need to force it, he had a pick for that. The drawer was open in a few minutes.

Inside he found a single manila envelope containing a form letter from a lawyer from Ghent.

He didn't know what this meant yet but he did know it was important.

Reid returned to the bedroom to arrange the body. He was sure he was in time to avoid the complications of rigor mortis. He worked to remove any signs of struggle, placing the Westland woman in a sleeping position in the bed and arranging the bedclothes to make it look possible she'd died in her sleep.

It would be some time before a post mortem could be held and find she'd been asphyxiated. Even then, they might not be certain that a second party was involved. By then he would be away with his million, maybe two if he could find the husband.

The visit had not been a waste of time; he had the letter. Something told him that for the right person this might be worth more than the two million he was chasing.

Day 4

Friday August 22nd

Chapter 48

The news would devastate Julia; Miles knew that. Yet he also knew he should be the one to tell her. It was better that it came from him rather than the shock of her hearing this from elsewhere.

He was standing in line at immigration at Chicago Oare Airport and because of the five-hour time difference it was still just 5 AM there. He was flight side and shouldn't be using the phone but there was reception and there were messages that could wait no longer.

After checking the messages he called Julia.

There was a long wait before she picked up.

"Julia. Are you all right? I didn't think you were going to answer."

"I didn't want to pick up."

"You're safe?"

"Yes. Craig is here. He has a room down the corridor. He keeps watch. Nothing to worry about. And your flight?"

"It was fine. But we were delayed getting a landing slot and now I'm in a line at immigration and it's not moving. And I have a new message from Reyas. *Meet in Albuquerque. Sandia Peak Tramway. 10.40 AMT.*"

"Not Austin?"

"He's made a switch. Don't ask me why. I now need to change my ticket."

"You'll get there in time?"

"I should be fine to get an early morning flight out there." Miles paused. "Listen, Julia, I have something to tell you and it's best you hear this from me."

"James?"

"Not James. But not good."

"What then?"

"When I landed, I checked the news feeds on my phone. There's a piece you need to know about. There's no good way of saying this. Peggy Westland has died."

Miles could sense the shock that Julia must be feeling. "She was well yesterday. What happened?"

"It says Peggy Westland, widow of well-known painter Richard Westland, died last night in her sleep in her apartment in Sloane Square. The body was discovered early next morning by her cleaner. Though the outcome of a post mortem is awaited, initial police investigations point to death from natural causes."

Julia sounded angry and shocked. "That can't be, Miles. That can't be."

Chapter 49

I'd never been the type before this but now I knew what paranoia was all about.

It was more than a game of cat and mouse. I was caught up in my very own dystopia. To everyone around me, the world had the unexceptional sheen of normality. To me, the world was filled with those who listened to and observed my every move.

The FBI guys were working me hard and working me well.

I was watched overnight on a rota basis – three hours of Jones, three hours of Michael, three hours of Philips.

Even then they were taking no chances. The phone in the hotel room had been disabled.

"Come on buddy. You might as well sleep. The phone's dead. You've got no way of sneaking out of here and getting a message out, so why not shut your eyes and give us all a break."

I had no sleep that night. It was too hot for sleep anyway. The air conditioning was noisy and no match for the eighty degree overnight temperature.

By morning I was exhausted.

Agent Craven came in. "OK, James, time to get up. It's show time. Time to play out your role as Charles

Harrington, computer nerd and delegate to the Comicom trade fair out at the Conference Centre."

I looked back, bleary-eyed, and didn't reply.

Craven turned to Philips, the last one on the rota to watch over me. "And what should Harrington be doing, Agent Philips?"

"Why, sir, he should be getting up, showering, getting dressed real smart, going down to breakfast to look over his itinerary for the day and getting ready to board the bus taking him out to the exhibition."

Craven smiled. "And the bus leaves in forty minutes." He then turned to me. "That's if you're still with us?"

I thought about Julia. I thought about Miles and what could happen to them both if I refused to play along. "OK. I hear you."

I showered and dressed. Craven left the room but Philips stayed. I wasn't going to be allowed privacy. "What do you think I'm going to do?"

Philips smiled back. "Just following the plan."

The plan had me seated at breakfast where I could be seen if anyone was watching and checking to see if I was following the expected routine of the trade fair attendee I was supposed to be. I ate the breakfast. I looked over my papers for the day.

When I looked around the room, Craven's agents could be seen here and there pretending otherwise but nonetheless observing my every move and with that came the paranoia. What if the assailant Craven was expecting was here and watching, planning how to take me out? From that point of view the level of protection was minimal. It wasn't that I was the bait in the trap so much as I was the pre-emptive sacrifice. Craven didn't care what happened to me as long as he smoked out his man.

It was the same on the bus taking the delegates to the exhibition. I sat on the outside seat, third row from the front, next to a rotund middle-aged man from Tennessee. We exchanged pleasantries about the heat in Austin at this time of year and then talked about what we were looking forward to at the Comicom trade fair.

I thought of asking him to get a message out for me, to ask him to tell the world I was being held against my will. But I had to decide against it. The paranoia hit home again. How did I know the man from Tennessee wasn't one of Craven' s men, one I hadn't seen before? No, that was a risk I couldn't take, not when I knew what might happen to Julia and Miles if I got this wrong.

It was the same at the exhibition. As I made my tour of the stands and stopped to take the expected interest here and there, I was sure my every step was being followed. I thought I recognised one of them from the plane but he was soon gone and I was left with the feeling that the others watching were there working as a team in such a way that none was close enough for long enough for me to be able to single them out.

I tried to move between the exhibition stands in as unpredictable a way as possible without giving them the idea I might be trying to lose them. I thought it might have worked when I came to a stand on SDRAM storage at the far end of the hall.

I was sure I must have lost them.

There, set against the wall, was a public phone box.

I would have less than a minute and I had no coins, no card. It would have to be a collect call. I was thinking fast.

Was there anyone here in the States who would accept a collect call from me? There was Malcolm Spencer who'd worked with me in radio in London and who'd taken a job out here. But I couldn't remember his number. Was there a way of getting the number from an operator?

My time was up.

A hand came down on my shoulder. It was Philips. He whispered, "Not thinking about the public phone, are we?"

I shook my head. "Just tired of walking round the stands."

"That's OK. I have a message that you're returning to the hotel. There's a bus out front in ten minutes."

The journey back to the hotel was like the journey out. I had no way of knowing if one or more of the business types on the bus were with Craven or not. I made the journey in silence.

Back at the hotel, the surveillance rota came back into action. Craven explained. "You lie low for the rest of the afternoon. Get some rest. You're back at it this evening."

Chapter 50

Miles reached the Sandia Peak Tramway outside Albuquerque with half an hour to spare. He hadn't slept much on the flight from Chicago and could feel the jet lag bite.

Luiz Reyas was nowhere to be seen.

There was tourism all year in the Sandia Mountains but at this time, with no snow, the area wasn't crowded. A group of Chinese waited in silence for the tramway car to wind its way down the four thousand feet precipice of the Sandia Mountain Range as the ascending companion car aimed for the top. It was a three-mile trip during which the tramway car lurched over two turrets connecting the three sections of cable on which it ran.

The downward traveling car was approaching. Miles looked up at the display board. The next departure was scheduled to leave in less than five minutes yet there was no sign of Reyas. Miles began to feel foolish that he'd travelled so far on such slender information.

The car arrived and half a dozen tourists clambered out. It was going to be a short turnaround. The Chinese tourist party boarded. The car was ready to go.

There was a voice behind Miles. "Please get in, Senor."

It was Reyas.

Miles stepped aboard. "Cutting it fine?"

Reyas replied, "You made it over OK?"

They spoke like host and guest with nothing that would be out of place to the casual listener. "The flight was smooth enough. Some delay in getting into Chicago. I had to change tickets there after clearing immigration but I made the connection here this morning with no problems."

The tramway car began its journey to the summit. Miles didn't want to admit to the vertigo he suffered from and made sure not to look down.

They didn't want to talk here and fell into silence as the ascent continued.

The air had begun to thin as they approached the first support turret at seven thousand feet. As the tramway car lurched as it crossed the turret, Miles could no longer hide his discomfort.

Reyas smiled. "It's like that. Nothing to worry about. Unless you get to thinking too much about what it's going to be like on the way down."

Miles took deep breaths. "I'll be OK."

The ride over the second turret was no better than that over the first. Miles fought back nausea as the tramway car lurched again on its way. When the tramway car shuddered to a stop at the summit, Miles lied. "That wasn't so bad."

Reyas was still smiling. "The charm of the English."

They disembarked and walked along a narrow path that threaded its way across the Sandia Crest. Reyas paused. They looked out across the vast expanse of the Rio Grande plain, ten thousand feet beneath them.

Reyas spoke quietly. "This place is sacred to the Pueblo. You can see why."

Fifty miles away, on the other side of the plain, a storm with forked lightning standing out against black cloud was playing out. It was like looking at events in another time and place where a less than benign god was making weather. Yet up here the late afternoon sun was shining.

Reyas did not look at Miles as he spoke. "This is a place of reckoning. Where the events of the past are spread out as if on the plain below us. Where you can touch them from the present. That's why I've come here. One of the reasons I've brought you here."

Miles was hesitant. "I don't have time for the past. I have a problem in the here and now. My brother is missing. I need to find him."

"Stay with me, Senor." Reyas was still staring at the distant storm. "This place informs me of my goal. What has set me apart in this life. How I can find a way to do what I've been raised to achieve."

They stood and watched the distant storm in silence.

After some minutes, Reyas spoke again. "I want you to know from the start, so there is no doubt, I am not a good man. It has been expected of me and I have killed."

Miles was defensive. "You don't have to tell me this."

"You need to know if you are to understand." Reyas was insistent. "The only way I remained true to the goal I was raised with was to get close to evil. To join a cartel. And to win their trust I have had to kill."

Reyas rolled back his right shirtsleeve to reveal over a hundred tattoo stars. "Senor. One for each man."

Miles tensed but tried not to show how much he was unprepared to be in the company of such a man. "You've had your reasons."

"They were not good men, the ones I killed. But they had wives and children and families and they should not have been lost to them this way. Yet this is the life I lead and this is as it is. I leave you to make sense of it or not, as you wish. And if you can make sense of it, we may have a deal."

"What kind of deal?"

"I share my world with you. You help me achieve my goal. A simple trade. One based on honour between two men who have a common cause."

Miles agreed – something he hoped he would not come to regret. He stretched out his hand. "You have my word."

Reyas took Miles' hand and squeezed it tight. "We have an agreement, Senor."

They went to the rooftop restaurant and ordered coffee. It was too early for alcohol yet the altitude still made Miles feel lightheaded. He knew he had to concentrate. "Ruiz, tell me why we're here."

The Mexican was preoccupied with his phone. "Excuse me, Senor. I must check to see if there is a signal." He smiled as he was able to pick up the information he wanted here in the restaurant. "Something I need to keep in contact with."

Miles repeated the question. "Why are we here?"

Reyas put the phone away. "I thought you would start, Senor. Tell me what happened in Florence. And why you have agreed to meet me after so long turning down my invitations to talk."

Miles was unsure how much he should tell this man. How could he trust someone who had killed so many times? But the logic of recent events and the urgency of the need to find James meant he knew he had to forget these doubts. "I couldn't see the value in letting you know what happened to Julia Blake."

"It is good you are now being honest."

Miles continued. "I was interested in what you could tell me about the drugs network in Mexico. Nothing else. As a good journalist, I discounted your interest in what happened to Julia as not relevant to the story I'm trying to break."

Reyas smiled. "And now you do?"

"Maybe. Maybe, after all, what happened in Florence is more important than I thought."

Miles told Reyas about what he and Julia had discovered in their investigation of the Pugot letter. He told him about the theft of Picasso's *Weeping Woman* and the copies made by Westland and he told him about the families who had received letters from Pugot's lawyer on his death.

Reyas listened. He gave a broad smile at the mention of *Weeping Woman*. "What you've told me confirms my greatest expectations. That you have told me this here on the Sandia is proof this is indeed a magical place. I've taken a giant step closer to realising my goal."

Miles was intrigued. "You need to tell me why."

The restaurant was empty. The party of Chinese tourists had long departed along one of the hiking trails yet Reyas still spoke so Miles could just hear. "Life in Mexico is not as it is here. The past is never absent. We live to right the wrongs of that past and this has been the purpose in my life."

Reyas told Miles about that past, how his great grand-father had been a prosperous rancher in Mexico in the early years of the twentieth century. He made his money by raiding the cattle herds in Texas and smuggling the animals across the border where he passed them off as local Mexican cattle. This was illegal but not immoral since many of the cattle roamed free. He was a good man and was well-respected. He mixed with bad people when he needed to smuggle the herds across the border but they also respected him for being good at what he did. He remained untainted. He rose above all that and became wealthy. As his wealth increased, he was feted by Mexican society and he became well thought of when he began using some of his wealth to help the poor.

Reyas leaned forward. "Until he was offered *Ui Giaconda*."

"The *Mona Lisa*?"

Reyas nodded. "He made this one great mistake and it ruined his life. He knew the painting had been stolen and when it was offered to him he was unable to resist. He wanted it that much. For him, it was the crowning achievement of his rise from humble origins to this peak of power and influence. To think he would be the owner of the most valuable painting in the world."

Reyas told how his great grandfather couldn't keep secret for long the fact that he owned the masterpiece. First he told his wife then his son, Reyas' grandfather, then close associates and then the men who helped him smuggle the cattle across the border. The knowledge would be safe with them. He could bask in the admiration of all those he'd told and this was as it was for a few years. Then the news broke. The *Mona Lisa* had been found in Italy. Reyas' great grandfather had been sold a worthless copy.

"From then on, he lost the respect of those around him." Reyas was finding it hard to control his emotions. "They questioned his judgment. How could he have been cheated out of such a large sum of money? Many of those around him had risked their lives to make that money and he'd wasted it. The questioning turned to loathing and hatred. His authority was shot. Others moved in on the cattle smuggling business. Within a few years the family was ruined, the Estate sold off and he died a broken man."

Miles had listened carefully. "What was his name?"

"Luiz Reyas."

"The same name as you."

"It is the tradition in my family. Each first son in each generation is called Luiz. That first son is raised to find a path to righting the wrongs visited on the family."

"Revenge?"

"If you want to call it that, Senor. Righting the wrongs is what we prefer to call it."

"Over so many years."

"Just as with the Pueblo, time does not come into this. It is about justice and there is no statute of limitations on that. You need to understand my journey. How I arrive at this moment."

Reyas spoke of his own life. About how he was raised as the eldest son in his generation to take up the goal of avenging the Reyas family and finding the ancestors of the perpetrators of the fraud that had ruined them. He spoke of the frustration of his father who'd been given the goal and who had taken it one step further in identifying an Argentinian, di Valfierno, as the perpetrator of the swindle. Yet the attempts to find the ancestors of di Valfierno had failed. He was traced to Buenos Aires but there the trail had remained cold. It had been a false name and the tracks had been well covered. As the next Luiz in the family, the youngster would have a fresh start. He might succeed where his father had failed. He immersed himself in the knowledge the Reyas family had on the *Mona Lisa* swindle. It wasn't much for all the efforts down the years. And he was immersed in the need to remove the sense of shame at having been tricked so easily that had blighted the family over all those years.

Reyas cleared his throat. "We had no wealth. There was nowhere for me to go but into the cartels. I am not proud of it. But it has brought me to where I am today."

He told of how, at the point when he thought he might never be able to take up the challenge his father had set for him, a chance comment from a dying man had given him hope. The man told him one of the players in Europe they supplied with drugs was also involved in illegal art. It was a long shot, he knew, but before he killed the man he got him to tell him that the cartel headed by El Romero was where the story about the art scams was centred and that one of those scams involved a stolen Picasso. Luiz had a reputation and thirty stars on his forearm by then and joined El Romero.

"I had to be careful and I took my time to win their trust but I found out more about the links with the European players. And all the time I was sifting through in my mind which of those players might be also involved in illegal art. The trouble was, it wasn't a short list. It seems that making money from drugs and having an interest in art is not mutually exclusive. I identified a dozen families spread throughout Russia, Germany, France and the UK who could have been involved. I needed more information and that's when I risked making contact with a journalist like you, Senor."

Miles interrupted. "I didn't think I was the only one you were in touch with."

"There are over ten like you who I hoped might help. I'd come a little way along the path but so much of it was on a single rumour from a dying man and I began to doubt if I was going to achieve anything more than my father. Now today you tell me about the theft of the Picasso and I understand."

"You're connecting the thefts of the *Mona Lisa* and Picasso's *Weeping Woman*?"

Reyas nodded. "More than that, I can see that both swindles were committed by the same family. I understand, Senor Blake, that those who commit the greatest crimes do not need to be clever and seldom are. There are only so many ways you can be successful in doing evil to others and benefiting from it yourself. And once these people know what succeeds they use it again, and again. So, you see the importance of what you've just told me here on Sandia Mountain?"

Miles chose his words carefully. "I must tell you I have information that may prove you're right. When Julia Blake was in Florence, she discovered an indication that Alessa Lando's family could have been involved in both thefts." Miles told Reyas about the copies of the paintings seen by Julia in Lucca.

Reyas gave a broad smile. "You understand now why I asked you here?"

"Yes, for the first time you know which family it was."

"Yes, Senor. What you have told me confirms that it is the Lando family who brought disgrace and humiliation to my family."

"It wouldn't be enough to convince my editor, let alone a jury."

"That doesn't matter, Senor. I was raised in the knowledge that one day the truth would be put before me and I would recognise it for what it is. I have just heard that truth. I now have a means of achieving my goal. I thank you from the bottom of my heart."

Miles had one more question. "Why Albuquerque? The mountain is not the only reason we're here, is it?"

Reyas smiled. "You are right, Senor. Everything I have said about this place is true. But there is another reason why I arranged for us to meet here. I follow a man. A devil."

"What man?"

"He works with El Romero. A German no one trusts. So, I am charged to follow him and report back to El Romero where this man goes and what he does. A man who kills from a list."

"Why do you call him a devil?"

"Because of what I have seen he can do."

"You say he works with El Romero?"

"Yes, but I know he doesn't work for him. He works for someone else but El Romero has not taken me into this confidence."

"And Albuquerque is a town on the German's list?"

"I believe it to be so."

"And where else has this man been?"

"San Diego. He drew a blank there and moved on to Austin. Before that I heard he was in Boston."

It was Miles' turn to be surprised by what he'd heard. The locations where the German had travelled matched the addresses to which the Pugot letters were sent. The conclusion was becoming inescapable. "I think I know what list this German is working to and who he's working for."

"Senor?"

"Those locations are the same as the addresses used by Pugot's lawyer to let families know who'd swindled them over the Picasso theft. Montgomery in Boston, Ravitz in San Diego, Davidson in Albuquerque. He's working for the Landos."

Reyas smiled. "I follow him yet I do not know this. If you are right, Senor, the German has an importance in achieving my goal I had not suspected. It is an important day, indeed."

"You now know who you're looking for?"

"Yes, but with these people a name is never enough, as my family found out. We had the di Valfierno name but could never find them. Before she was Alessa Lando, she was called something else. Now, she'll have changed her name again. But with the German, we have a link to her."

"The German, he has a name?"

"Heller. Wolfgang Heller."

Chapter 51

For DI Reid it was time to collect. He wanted the two million but knew he should be realistic. After he'd gone that far with the Westland woman, time was short.

So, he didn't know where James Blake was. What did that matter? He knew where the wife was. The one million he could collect for turning her in would be a good enough place to start.

And he had the letter. It could be worth more than the missing million.

Sergeant Billy Smith would not do for this. This was in a different league. He needed to go to the source, to the one who, when Reid made those initial background checks, he was told he needed to contact to get the reward.

Reid called Retired Chief Superintendent Giles Cleary, once a powerful figure with a national profile, now what you would call a man with an influential presence, someone not used to giving attention to a mere DI like Reid. It was strange to think that anyone looking at this from the outside would conclude that what they were to talk about was corrupt – when looked at from the inside this was just normal business.

The call was answered and Cleary was defensive. "How did you get this number?"

Reid insisted. "I was told I could use this number if I got a result."

"You have a result?"

"Yes, I've found one of the targets. I'm claiming the reward."

"Let's meet."

Reid memorised the address. It was in the East End, far enough from Canary Wharf to be an unknown quantity. It was nearby. He could be there in ten minutes.

He should have taken more time to check it out. The address turned out to be a warehouse that couldn't have been in use for fifty years or more. As he walked in he was captured by three men and held by two of them while their leader faced him.

The leader was a stocky Italian with piercing eyes. He was shouting in poor English. "The location. What is the location?"

Reid was finding it difficult to speak. Adrenalin was rushing through his blood. He couldn't think straight.

Why were they not covering their faces? This did not look good.

He managed to get the first few words out before they hit him. "I'm police. You don't want to be hunted for assaulting a British police officer."

A giant ringed fist smashed into his face, breaking his teeth. "The location. We need the location."

Reid was still playing it brave. "I need the reward."

The fist crashed again into Reid's face. "The location."

They began to beat him with iron bars. The pain was so acute he was unable to tell them anything. His screams were the only sounds made.

Until they stopped.

The Italian approached him again. "One last time, we need the location."

Through broken teeth, Reid pleaded for his life. "I have something you need. A letter."

"Give me the letter."

"I don't have it here. Let me go and I'll take you to it."

The Italian laughed. "Search him."

It was another mistake. The letter was in his jacket pocket. They removed it and the iron bar treatment began again.

He only wanted the pain to stop. Reid blurted it out. "Allegro Hotel. Allegro Hotel."

"How many?"

"The woman. Just her."

"You don't have the man?"

"I don't have him."

The Italian took a pace back and admired his handi-work. "Do you know who I am?"

Reid shook his bleeding head.

The Italian continued. "My name is Luigi Bandini. I work for Alessa Lando. A man like you should know these things."

Reid knew there was only one reason why he would be told this.

It wasn't right that his dreams should end like this. There was no justice in the world. He'd seen and tasted the life he thought was going to be his – the bright sunshine, the warm wash of wealth, the beautiful women, all that he'd been destined to possess.

Bandini gave a signal to one of his men. "Finish it."

He pulled out a gun. It was pressed to Reid's temple.
The gun fired.
Reid was gone.

Chapter 52

The tramway car was empty when Miles and Luiz Reyas boarded for the descent from Sandia Mountain. They were the only passengers since the party of Chinese had not returned from the nature trail.

The tramway car lurched and started the descent. Miles tried to think of something other than the time it would take to make it back down.

Since they were alone, they could talk without fear of being overheard. Miles concentrated his mind on the German. "You followed Heller here from Austin?"

Reyas pulled his phone from his pocket. "Yes, Senor. And I have help in that matter. This tells me where he goes." He showed Miles the map display with its blinking blue pin.

Miles now knew the reason why the Mexican was so concerned to keep checking the phone. "So, you know where he is, now?"

"Indeed. When he arrived in Albuquerque, he headed for a motel and booked in. He's been there since. He's been sleeping or preparing himself for what's coming next. The signal has not been moving."

"You took a risk in coming up here. You could have lost him."

"It was important that we met at this place. So you would know I am not the man I seem to be. So you would believe me." Reyas looked again at the phone. "And he still has not moved. He remains at the motel. It was a risk worth taking, then."

Miles wanted to keep talking, to avoid thinking about the precipitous drop beneath the cable car. "So, Heller came here from Austin."

"He has unfinished business there. And there is something more you should know, Senor. One of the families you said was involved with the *Weeping Woman* swindle, Ravitz, is the reason Heller went to Austin."

"Elmore Ravitz. We had him located in San Diego."

"He was moved from there."

"You know some say Ravitz is future presidential material."

"Then, Senor, that would explain the security at the house on Town Lake. I followed Heller there. I saw him looking the place over and then walking away."

Miles wanted to know more but the vertigo induced by the descent was about to overcome him. The judder as the tramway car passed over the first and then the second turret was no worse than on the ascent except that the mere fact of going down made this all the more frightening. He was trying not to look down, trying to eliminate from his mind the gnawing fact someone had told him years before but which now infiltrated his thoughts: if you look at the face of the mountain you can see wreckage from the Boeing 747 crash of the 1950s – the terrain is so inaccessible that much of the wreckage remains.

Reyas was unaffected by the descent. "TWA Canyon, Senor. It should not be that frightening, not for a man of your stature." He paused and then continued. "Another thing, Senor. In Austin, the German showed interest in an Englishman staying in the Warren Richardson Hotel. I followed him there. I watched as he looked the man over."

Miles was grateful to take his mind off the descent once more. "Describe him."

"The man in the hotel?"

Miles nodded.

"Like you, Senor. Enough like you to be your brother."

Miles called up a photo of James from his phone.

Reyas smiled. "Yes, Senor. That's him."

They had reached the bottom of the descent and the tramway car lurched to a halt.

Miles climbed out onto secure, flat earth and made no comment about his relief at having made it back down.

His only thought was to head for Austin to find James.

Reyas was insistent they should stay on the trail of Heller.

In the event, it came down to the same thing.

They were in downtown Albuquerque, preparing to go out to the motel where Heller was staying when the truth became clear.

The blue pin on Reyas' phone that tracked Heller's movements showed he was active and moving quickly. It didn't take long to work out that the German's direction of travel led to the airport.

Reyas was troubled. "He's leaving Albuquerque. It means only one thing. He's heading back to Austin."

"Why would he do that when he's achieved nothing here?"

"That I don't know, Senor. Just that we need to go now if we are not to lose him."

They hailed a taxi and headed for the airport. Halfway there, the blue pin on the display disappeared.

"He's turned the phone off." Reyas was shocked. "Which means…"

"He's airborne."

Matters got worse when they reached the airport. Heller had planned well. Not only had he arranged his trip to minimise the time he would need to wait before his flight to Austin, he'd made sure there was a four hour wait for the next flight in case anyone was following.

Then came the bad news. The flight wasn't direct. Miles and Reyas would have to go via Phoenix. That, and the wait to leave Albuquerque, put them well behind Heller.

As they waited in the departure lounge, what Heller had done in Albuquerque became clear. A TV reporter was taking viewers through the details of a local crime. It was motiveless. The dead man had been walking dogs in the Casa District when he'd been stabbed. Miles doubled his attention as he heard the name of the man who had died.

He turned to Reyas. "Stephen B Davidson. One of the recipients of the Pugot letter. It was Heller."

Reyas looked again at the phone. "Nothing, not even this, is foolproof, then, Senor."

Miles was puzzled. "Heller's phone didn't leave the motel room. But he did. Why would he do that?"

"Something unforeseen. Something about the way he worked that meant there was no place for the phone."

"Or he forgot it."

"I doubt it, Senor. A man like that has a reason for everything. Maybe he was just being careful and left it there while he made the hit."

Miles frowned. "However it happened, he's ahead of the game. He has a four hour head start on us."

It got worse. There was further delay at Phoenix when the plane they were due to board reported mechanical failure. The hope was that when they reached Austin the next morning they would be able to pick up Heller once more from his phone signal.

Chapter 53

Julia was impressed with Martin Craig.

He knew he was putting himself in danger by protecting her yet he was calm and collected and accepting of what Miles had told him even though he must have known this wasn't even a quarter of the truth. She didn't like the idea of Craig putting himself in harm's way without knowing what kind of threat he was facing.

That was both the problem she now faced and the reason why Miles had been economical with the truth. Was there risk if Craig knew the whole story?

It came down to a matter of instinct. Was he a man she could trust?

Craig had taken her through the procedure. He was keen to respect her privacy at the same time as he offered protection. His room in the hotel was on the same corridor and from there he could keep watch over her. He gave her a pager linked to his own. If she had a concern of any kind, for any reason, she should use the pager. She should only leave the hotel if he was with her. If she saw anyone suspicious, she should go back to her room and alert him. If they were followed she should make for her room and bring them along the corridor past Craig's room, pressing the pager call button and knocking on the door as she went past. He would do the rest.

He gave her these instructions in such a matter of fact way that she began to feel more at ease just hearing him tell her about them.

She was warming to his cool assurance. Her instinct told her to tell him more.

They were seated downstairs in a quiet area of the lobby. There was no one near and Julia thought they should talk. "Miles didn't tell you everything."

Craig wasn't fazed. "My clients seldom do. I don't ask. It's simpler that way. The protection needed is the same in the end. Nine times out of ten, the risk is overestimated in any case."

She was impressed again by his calmness. "You might need to know what we're facing is no ordinary threat."

"Then why not go to the police?"

"That's not possible."

He smiled. "And that's why I'm here."

"It's a long story."

"If you feel I need to know, tell me."

Craig listened as Julia told him what had happened in recent days and in her past. She made him aware of the level of the threat from Italy. She told him of her pain at not knowing where they'd taken James.

He asked few questions and when she finished he had just two words to say. "I understand."

At dinner in the hotel later that evening Julia was again approached by the hotel manager who was astonished when she answered his question about her proof of identification by showing him the passport in the name of Elizabeth Meredith that Miles had obtained. He scrutinised it in detail but could find nothing to fault. "Your husband, Mr. Meredith, gave you this?"

Julia shook her head. "No, he's still away on business. My brother brought it to me."

"And where is your brother?"

"He's right here." Craig, who was sitting opposite Julia, was introduced to the manager who expressed further surprise. "Excuse me, sir, I had not made the connection."

Craig smiled. "It's a pleasure to be able to keep my sister company, I'm sure you understand."

The manager left without mentioning that having sight of the passport now made no difference since he'd already long before reported the matter to the police.

Julia felt secure having Craig to protect her but she knew a long night lay ahead without knowing where Jim was.

After a fruitless day at the Comicom fair and a wasted evening of paranoia in the bar of the Warren Richardson acting as bait for the operative Craven was so sure would appear, I made another attempt to have it out with him.

"What makes you so sure he's going to show?"

"Enough, James. Why can't you accept that we're expert at what we do and if we say it's only a matter of time before the guy shows you should believe us?"

"Because it's the 'just a matter of time' part of this I don't get. Meanwhile, I have to take on trust that you're looking after Julia's safety."

He tried to look and sound convincing but I knew I shouldn't believe a word he was saying.

"Look, as I've told you more than once, James, you can trust us. Why can't you accept this simple fact?"

"You're promising me you have her under your protection in London?"

"James, you have my absolute assurance that's the case."

"Let me talk to her then."

"You know we have an agreement not to allow that. I can't think you want to go back on our agreement."

I thought about Miles and what Craven had in mind for him if I didn't continue to co-operate, and I thought about Julia and the possibility that Craven's intentions might turn hostile towards her and I backed down. "OK. So, how long do you expect this show to go on?"

He smiled. "As long as it takes." He turned to Agent Miller who'd sat with me once more during the evening's vigil. "We're in no hurry, are we, Debbie?"

She replied without a smile. "Just as you want it, sir."

Craven turned back to me. "He'll show. As I told you, it's only a matter of time and we have all the time in the world."

He waved a hand and Agent Philips, the first on the rota as my overnight guard, stepped forward. "Time to get some rest, James. Tomorrow could be the big day."

Day 5

Friday August 23rd

Chapter 54

It was unfortunate that Wolfgang Heller would have to resort to something this direct on his return to Austin but they'd left him no choice – with such levels of security surrounding Ravitz the course of action he was about to take was inevitable.

After all, as one of the god-fearing of this world he had a right to find a way past such restrictions by whatever means he had at his disposal.

That was justification enough to depart from his normal methods. He liked to see the look in the eyes of those he dispatched, to make sure they understood the power of the man who'd brought this end to their lives, but, alas, it would have to be different this time.

El Romero was good for something, at least. He had enemies that Heller had found it easy to work with – men like Johnny Rivenza. He'd obtained the plastic explosive and detonators at short notice on the Tijuana black market, had sent them across the border with one of his drugs mules and delivered the merchandise to Heller in Austin. It was something El Romero would never have had the courage to do.

Building the weapons would not be a problem. Apt that here they called them improvised explosive devices, IEDs. He would draw on the counter insurgency training he'd received in an earlier life. He knew how to use the two smart phones he'd just bought as the timers. He smiled at the thought of how appropriate it was that advances in technology made such features available to anyone. He'd always liked plastic explosives, the way he could mould it to take up the shape he wanted.

That was important. In this heat, there was no question of concealing the explosive under a jacket. He would have to mould it around his body and wear it under a shirt. The oppressive heat of this place would be intensified and hard to bear without giving away what he was concealing but he would call on the power of the tantric energy at the heart of his control over the world and no one would know.

The trip to Albuquerque had served him well. His enemies in the FBI had been kept waiting for anything to happen here in Austin. They were expecting a strike on the Englishman at the hotel but not on the Ravitz compound. He was about to give them both. But first, there was work to be done.

While in Albuquerque he'd visited a clothing ware-house just outside town. It was remarkable, he thought, that you could purchase just about anything in this country, no questions asked, so long as you had the money. He'd bought a contract police uniform with all the necessary additions and, trying it on now in the back of the vehicle he'd hired and looking at himself in the driver mirror, he thought it looked good on him. More than that, he thought it made him look authoritative.

That was the idea. Heller knew that in this country there was a multitude of companies offering policing services – protecting schools, universities, shopping malls and public buildings – many armed, most working for small unregulated companies. In the protection measures taken at Town Lake to safeguard his targets it was no different. When he'd checked out the compound, he'd observed that alongside the men from the FBI was private uniformed security from more than one company. He'd also observed the comings and goings taking place as men checked off shift and others came in for work. He'd followed one of the men home. He'd broken the man's neck and taken his security pass. The man would not report for duty again. It didn't matter now. Heller would be reporting in his place.

He knew better than to pretend to be the man he'd just killed or to present himself in the man's uniform. There was too great a risk that one of the man's colleagues would notice that Heller didn't look anything like the man he'd replaced. No, this was better. He would swipe his way into the compound using the dead man's security card. That was the identity check. Once cleared, there would not be any others. If challenged at some other time when he was within the compound, he would say he was from a new security company, hired to increase the numbers. Yet he knew that was unlikely – if you encounter an authoritative man in a uniform who looks as if he belongs you have no reason to challenge him.

All it took was the courage to walk into the Ravitz compound in the full light of day and look as if he belonged. It might be a problem for most men but Heller knew he wasn't like most men. Courage would not fail him.

It would help that this was early morning, 6.30 AM, when the concentration of those who had been on duty all night was at its lowest, when their thoughts had turned to going home as the morning shift arrived.

He left the hire vehicle a short distance from the front entrance of the compound and walked towards the gatehouse. The guard there was not FBI, he was private security like himself. Heller could see him looking at him with care as he approached.

For this to work, he needed to know where the swipe card entry/exit lock was housed, so he would not arouse suspicion by being seen to be searching for it. He was in luck. An FBI agent was exiting. There was the machine, on the far side of the entrance area. The FBI man was talking with the security guard in the gatehouse, distracting him.

"Everything in order?"

"Yes, sir. Everything's clear."

The FBI agent nodded as his path crossed Heller's. Heller nodded back and walked on towards the swipe card entry/exit lock. He pulled out the dead man's card and swiped it through. The door opened and with a nod from the guard in the gatehouse, Heller was in.

He knew not to rush but to move with purpose. This was difficult since he didn't know the place on the inside. There was a long corridor with windows out onto a garden area with well-kept shrubs. He needed to get to the end of the corridor to be nearer to the accommodation area. Just past halfway the door at the end of the corridor opened. A uniformed guard from the same company as the guard he'd killed walked towards him.

The guard approached but did no more than give a nod of acknowledgment as their paths crossed. Heller did not nod back. It was as things should be when you have authority.

Passing through the doorway at the end of the corridor he was now close to the family accommodation. The power of the explosive was such that he knew he wouldn't have to be that close. The twelve pounds of plastic explosive he'd moulded round his ribs and concealed beneath the uniform shirt was hot and sticky but had not been detected. It was enough for two bombs to blow this place apart.

The heavy security guarding the Ravitz family would be a little way off yet. But here, deep inside the compound but not yet that close to the family, uniformed guards were seldom deployed since no one was supposed to be able to get this far. This was the perfect position. The brute power of the explosives he had with him would destroy the whole area and everyone in it.

He found an unlocked cupboard situated halfway along the next corridor. It was used to house cleaning equipment and supplies. He stepped inside and closed the door behind him.

The security guard shirt was removed and Heller pulled out the materials for the IEDs. He divided the explosive into two six-pound blocks, shaped each to maximise the explosive impact and armed both detonators. He then attached the smart phones. He set the first to detonate in fifty-five minutes and the second to detonate after one hour and thirty-five minutes. The difference was the time it would take for the rescue and support teams to get into place. The second IED would take care of them.

He looked over the cupboard interior as he prepared to leave. The first IED was well concealed under a supply of paper towel rolls. It was unlikely they would be disturbed before they were needed at cleaning time later in the day.

He put on the shirt and rebuttoned it. It was now time for the difficult part, the planting of the second bomb. He would have to carry it in its assembled form beneath his shirt and accept a greater chance of its being seen. Yet, if he held his left arm across his stomach as he walked, it wasn't noticeable, given that he'd shaped it to lie flat beneath the shirt.

He emerged from the cupboard and ventured out into the corridor.

A twelve-year-old girl came round the corner and skipped towards him.

It was a child. This couldn't be. He resolved to stay calm. "You look happy, young girl."

She smiled back. "That's because I am happy."

"You can tell me the reason. I won't spread it about."

"I'm not telling you."

"A boy. You met a boy!"

She smiled again. "How did you guess? His name's Jimi and he's sweet. His daddy is a guard just like you."

Heller patted her on the head. "It's good to hear. What's your name?"

The girl looked up at him. "It's Jenny. Jenny Ravitz. And you're new here."

"Officer Merrill. But you can call me Larry. Leonard, really, but Larry is what everyone knows me as."

"You're here to keep us safe."

"Yes, Jenny. And I must complete my patrol."

"Bye, Larry."

Jenny Ravitz ran off along the corridor.

228

Heller knew this was no time to be sentimental. After all, they had forced him into this, forced him to use imprecise methods like this when, for God's sake, children would be involved. It was true, every word of it. These people had no courage, no honour, hiding behind children. It made him angrier than ever.

He made his way back towards the gatehouse. What was needed was a place to leave the second IED close enough to the gatehouse to maximise casualties yet somewhere it would not be seen. No location had suggested itself on the way in.

An FBI agent was approaching and for a moment Heller thought he would have to deal with the man as it seemed from his body language that he was about to stop him and ask for identification, yet the moment passed as the agent walked past with a nod of reassurance. Heller's sense of authority had won the day again.

Then he saw it. A stainless steel stand used to support a large vase of flowers. It was hollow at the back. It was another sign of the lack of quality in this country – why complete the back of a structure that no one would see?

Heller checked for security cameras in the corridor. He could see none. Nevertheless, in case he was being viewed, he made it look as if he was inspecting the area, checking it out as part of his job. Once out of sight behind the stand, he acted quickly. Here was an ideal space to conceal the second IED. He attached the primed detonator to the remainder of the plastic explosive that he'd pulled out from under his shirt.

He walked on towards the gatehouse. Would the fact he was about to check out after being in the compound for so short a time lead the guard there to trigger the alarm?

If he were in charge of security here it would be the kind of thing he would be looking for. Yet those who have themselves convinced their security is impregnable, as he was sure was the case here, were capable of overlooking such matters. He knew this was a weakness of his whole plan and he'd put much thought into how to overcome it. The answer, when it came to him, was so straightforward that he chastised himself for not having seen it sooner – make a point of leaving in plain sight and have a good reason for it.

The guard looked up at him as he approached the gatehouse.

Heller smiled and took his time. "You're not going to believe this. I have to swipe out."

The guard remembered him. "You been here, what, thirty minutes?"

"The company's got staffing issues. Three guys didn't show today and there's a VIP protection job downtown they have to cover. They've called me back to base."

The guard smiled. "Nothing you could say could amaze me. I've heard it all. How can these guys expect to run a professional service on a shoestring?"

"And we have to fill in the gaps."

The guard looked over towards the swipe card entry/exit lock. "You're out of here, buddy."

Heller swiped the card, thanked the guard and walked slowly away from the compound. It would be good to get out of the uniform once he reached the hire vehicle.

He had forty-five minutes before the first explosion.

As he drove away, Heller listened to Wagner. *Parsifal* again seemed right at this moment. Why was this the music he returned to above all other?

There would be a surveillance video showing him entering and leaving the compound. They would not see much – a man in a uniform with a cap covering most of his face. In any case, if his plan worked, as he knew it would, no one would find the video machine in the wreckage.

He found his thoughts returning to the girl.

Jenny would die.

He was alarmed he should be having doubts about this, that he'd even remembered her name. He convinced himself it wasn't his fault that she was there, that his enemies were depraved in hiding the target behind a mere child. Yet there were disturbing feelings about this he couldn't shake off. He turned up the volume of the music and let his mind drift. The heroism and certainty of men who did what they needed to do to be true to themselves like him was returning.

Heller glanced at his watch. Twenty minutes before the first IED detonated. Time to meet Mordini and prepare to take down the Englishman they so wanted him to target.

Chapter 55

Her parents would kill her if they knew what she was doing.

Jenny Ravitz waited to make her move until the FBI agent guarding them had been called away on some matter by her mother. She made her way into the corridor with the windows overlooking the garden at the rear of the compound and slipped the catch on the French doors.

She half-expected an alarm to sound since the security they had surrounded the family with was tight but this was a chance worth taking. How else was she going to get to see Jimi, the son of the guard she'd met when his father had brought him to work with him? If she set off an alarm she would get no more than a lecture for breaking the rules laid down by her father and mother, that the only time she should ever leave the building was when she was escorted to school by security and that even hadn't been arranged yet. She'd seen the security men using the door on their patrol of the garden and she hadn't seen them do anything to disable an alarm – they came in twos with one staying inside to re-engage the catch while the other went outside. All in all, it was a chance worth taking.

There was no alarm. She walked out through the French doors and made her way to the far side of the garden. There was a wire fence running alongside a line of Leland cypress trees that formed a dense, green barrier to the world outside. Jenny squeezed under the fence and found her way through the foliage. It was so compact she thought she might not make it through but then she saw clear sunlight and made her way onto the Lakeshore where Jimi was waiting.

He smiled as he saw her making her way out of the greenery. "You made it!"

"Don't say I haven't gone the extra mile to be here, Jimi Bancroft."

Fourteen-year-old Jimi was imagining himself as the male lead in the movie he'd seen the night before and was playing it cool. "That's OK, Jenny. Let's walk."

They held hands and began to walk along the lakeshore, listening to the waves from a passing pleasure steamer lap at their feet.

They heard it first – a deafening sound.

Then they turned and watched in horror as the rear of the compound was engulfed in an explosion of fire and light and disintegration. Debris, thrown hundreds of feet into the air as if it had been caught up in a tornado, was flung back to earth as morbid rain.

The family area where her mother and father were housed, the place from which she'd just absconded, was demolished, destroyed.

Jenny started to run towards the explosion. "I have to see if they're safe!"

Jimi pulled her back. He held her as tears welled in her eyes.

His voice was shaking. "You can't go back there. There's nothing anyone can do now."

Chapter 56

Early morning breakfast in the hotel restaurant wasn't given the same level of importance as the evening stints in the bar but it was part of the plan to present me as bait just the same. Craven told me he didn't care what time of day or night he caught his man so long as he succeeded.

Debbie Miller was with me, sharing breakfast.

I glanced around the room and saw the expected crowd – business types, most attending the trade fair, Craven and five, maybe six, of his men trying to look inconspicuous.

Then I saw him. He was a man I'd seen before with a face I couldn't forget – Giuseppe Mordini, one of the Lando men who worked for Alessa Lando in Florence, the fat man who'd tried to kill me on the London Underground.

I thought he'd gone to jail with the majority of the Lando family.

Yet here he was.

I turned to speak to Debbie but she didn't get time to listen to what I was about to say.

Craven and his men were on the move, Debbie with them. She shouted something as she headed for the exit with the other agents. "Town Lake. They've hit the compound."

I looked back towards Mordini. A tall, blonde-haired German was by his side. I did not need to question who this was. His look, his whole bearing told me this was the assailant Craven had put so much effort into trying to trap.

He eyed me with an intensity that left no doubt he was about to strike.

The trap had been successful. I had flushed out the assailant. The problem was Craven and his men were no longer here.

And this man with Mordini had known all along this was going to happen.

Chapter 57

For Wolfgang Heller, everything was going according to plan.

He'd met Giuseppe Mordini and gone with him to the *Warren Richardson Hotel* with three minutes to spare, three minutes before the first of the IEDs he'd positioned inside the Town Lake compound was due to detonate, leaving not enough time for anyone here to react to his presence.

He looked at his watch and thought how remarkable the synchronisation between everyday timing devices was. The detonation would take place now. He breathed a self-satisfied sigh. The enemies in the hotel would be getting the emergency messages on their mobile devices in a matter of minutes.

Yes, here the messages came. The look of anguish, bewilderment and terror as the truth dawned that the compound and with it the prize they were meant to protect had been hit.

He watched his enemies rushing from the room, trying their best not to descend into outright disarray, leaving the stage for Heller, just as he'd planned.

There was the Englishman. It was strange that Matteo placed such a high price on his head when the man looked as weak and degenerate as everyone else here. Though he did none of this in the expectation of personal reward and would have done it anyway out of loyalty, he determined to take the million on offer.

Heller reached into his jacket pocket and handled the gun. It was remarkable that in this country you could walk in off the street and buy a semi-automatic pistol that would deliver twenty rounds in under a minute.

It would not be subtle and it would not be satisfying but another name on his list would be crossed off. The Englishmen would be dead. There would be no difficulty in escaping given the pandemonium caused by the Town Lake explosion.

Chapter 58

Miles Blake entered the hotel restaurant with Luiz Reyas just as it was emptying.

A well-dressed man pushed past them. "Out of the way. This is an emergency."

They let the man pass and pressed on.

They had arrived in Austin cursing the delay at Phoenix and concerned that they'd lost contact with Wolfgang Heller. Miles' first concern had been to be taken to James and Reyas had taken him straight to the Warren Richardson.

Inside the restaurant, Miles had just a few seconds to weigh up what he found.

Who were the key players? Why was no one else here responding to the emergency, whatever it was?

As Miles scanned the room he first picked out his brother James seated on a stool at the breakfast bar. He was looking with shocked recognition at an Italian seated next to a tall blonde German. The Italian was Giuseppe Mordini, known to Miles from the events in Florence. The German pulled an automatic pistol from his jacket pocket.

From the alignment of these players, James was the target.

Luiz Reyas picked up one of the breakfast bar stools and hurled it at Mordini and the German. As it clattered into them, the pistol was knocked from the blonde man's grip.

Reyas shouted, "It's Heller. Get your brother out of here."

Chapter 59

Miles rushed towards me and grabbed my arm. "Jim. Get out of here!"

"Miles, what are you doing here?"

His reply was a single word. "Run!"

Miles led me towards the exit and down the stairs into the hotel lobby. We were followed by the Mexican who came in with Miles.

"They will not be delayed long, Senor. We have a few seconds head-start at most."

We pushed through the doors at the hotel front entrance and made it out into the heat of the street.

A black parking attendant in a bellboy uniform had just taken the keys from an elderly couple arriving at the hotel. The attendant was about to get into the Land Rover and drive it to the underground parking lot when Reyas ran up to him and did no more than raise his right forearm and pull back his shirt-sleeve. One sight of the multitude of star tattoos that Reyas revealed left no doubt what was required. With widened eyes, the attendant handed over the keys.

Miles was first to the driver's door and clambered in. Reyas took the front passenger seat and gave Miles the keys. There was just enough time for me to climb into the back seat before Miles drew away.

I looked behind and could see the reason Miles had not waited a moment longer. Giuseppe Mordini and the tall German, the pistol back in his hand, had made it onto the street. The gun was now being held at the temple of a thirty-year-old dressed in a Florida shirt who had arrived to find himself in the wrong place at the wrong time. He handed over the keys to his Ferrari sports. He was pushed to the floor as Mordini and the German took the vehicle.

I was thinking, if our escape depended on speed, a competition between Land Rover and Ferrari would have just one outcome.

There was no prospect of turning. The way forward was a long downward slope into the hotel underground parking lot. Miles powered the Land Rover down the ramp and turned at the bottom to enter the parking lot, the tires squealing on the smooth concrete floor. A few seconds later we could hear burning rubber behind us. I looked back. They were no more than fifty yards away and were closing.

The parking lot was built as a downward spiral on two levels with parking on each level. We would have to thread our way down to the basement level before climbing up again to find the ramp leading to the exit onto the street at the rear of the hotel.

Miles was out of breath and concentrating on driving but he was able to smuggle out a few words. "Jim. This is Luiz Reyas. A man you should trust."

There was no time for anything more than a short look of recognition between us as we negotiated a sudden sharp bend.

As we pulled out of the bend, I had just one question for Miles. "Is Julia safe? Is she out of danger?"

Miles shouted back. "She's OK. She's safe. I made sure she's looked after. Don't worry about this now."

"Back in the hotel bar. I recognised Mordini. But who is that with him?"

Miles shouted back. "It's Heller. Wolfgang Heller. All you need to know right now is he'll stop at nothing to kill you."

The Ferrari was no better than the Land Rover in this confined space and we kept our lead. When we caught sight of them as we began the climb back up from basement level, I could see that the German had the passenger seat window open and was preparing to fire if he could get a long enough sighting of us.

The tires squealed at deafening volume as we rounded the last corner on the way back up and entered the long ramp leading to the street. Would we make it to the top of the ramp before Mordini and Heller closed in and the German could get a clean shot at us?

As we reached the exit, a shot rang out. The bullet shattered the rear window of the Land Rover. Had I been sitting on the other side of the rear passenger seat I would have been hit but now the significant result was that the back seat was filled with broken glass.

We were lucky. The bullet travelled on but missed Miles and Reyas, exiting through and breaking a second window as it continued its trajectory.

Miles shouted. "Everyone all right?"

I shouted back. "I'm not hit."

Reyas opened his palms to say he was unharmed.

On the street, we pulled out onto North Congress Avenue just ahead of a delivery truck, causing the driver to brake and curse Miles' driving. For a moment, the stalled truck blocked the exit of Mordini and Heller in the chasing Ferrari. We made the most of this small advantage by making our way along North Congress and taking a right onto West 6th Street where the one-way traffic was moving at speed.

Miles pushed the Land Rover to the maximum in the hope we would get away, taking chances overtaking and undertaking slower moving traffic. For a while we thought we might make it.

Then Miles spotted the Ferrari in his driver mirror. "They're behind us and closing."

I looked back through the now-open rear window and could see Heller holding the gun out of the Ferrari passenger window, taking aim at us.

Miles threw the Land Rover into a sharp left that took us off West 6th and onto Baylor Street, a side street leading to West 5th. Behind us the Ferrari made the same turn and began closing with Heller again taking aim. Halfway along Baylor, at the junction with West 5th, the traffic lights were red and staying that way.

We did not have to make a choice at the lights.

Behind us Mordini and Heller were closer now. Heller took aim once more and fired. We felt the Land Rover lurch as the rear passenger tire was hit.

As Miles fought to keep enough control to steer the Land Rover, we crashed through the intersection and avoided collision with the onrushing vehicles on 5th only because the startled oncomers switched lanes and made drastic corrections to their plans. I just had time see a pickup truck and a coupe make a glancing collision that sent both vehicles spinning.

Miles had no real control. Still traveling at high speed, the Land Rover had taken up a trajectory of its own.

He stabbed the brakes and there was no response. He shouted, "Brakes are gone!"

The Land Rover exited Baylor and crossed West 5th on a forty-five degree path that took it through the parking lot of a brown tile roofed restaurant standing close to the *Consulado General de Mexico* building,

Beyond the parking lot stood a tall, dilapidated, graffiti-covered building clad in corrugated iron sheeting, sides and roof. The direction of travel meant that the Land Rover was going to run straight into the side of the building.

Reyas braced himself in the front passenger seat by bending double and clasping his hands over his head. When Miles did the same, I followed suit in the back passenger seat.

The Land Rover crashed into the graffiti-covered wall in a deafening rage of twisted metal and broken glass. The corrugated iron sheeting crumpled, deformed like crazy, screamed out loud, twisted into an improbable shape and saved our lives. The relentlessness of our forward motion had been turned into a strange stillness by the enormity of the energy absorbed by the deforming wall.

There was a moment of silence. Everything had come to a stop.

We had survived the crash.

Then the reality of the situation seeped back in.

Mordini and Heller would be on us if we didn't get out of the wrecked vehicle and get moving.

Chapter 60

Agent Craven cursed the decision he'd taken to get to the Town Lake compound by his own route when the rest of his team had insisted on going straight through town.

These things happened when you were responding to disaster. No matter how good the training, even experienced agents were affected in the heat of the moment.

The report that the compound housing the Ravitz family had been attacked while the majority of his team had been involved in the sting at the hotel designed to catch the perpetrator had come as a body blow. It would not be easy to explain and with that came the risk that the whole purpose of being here and playing the game out like this might unravel.

The drugs trade out of Mexico that had served the Ravitz family in the past and Craven's own involvement now would become known. He and most of his team would go to prison.

As if that wasn't bad enough, he was now stuck in a tailback on a road you could depend on to be clear most of the day. A twenty-wheel delivery truck had broken down on a narrow section and there was no way through.

He didn't like doing this. Everything he did was aimed at being covert, at not attracting attention.

Craven pulled out the emergency light unit and placed it onto the roof of his vehicle. He activated the flashing blue light and siren and began shunting the vehicle ahead. The irate driver leaned out of the off-side window and shouted back, "Hey, buddy!"

Craven pointed to the flashing light. "Emergency! Pull over and make space."

There was just enough room to turn once the driver ahead had responded. Craven worked his way onto the opposite lane, turned and began to retrace his path.

He would be at least fifteen minutes late. By the time he got out to the compound the show would be over. He should have listened to Debbie Miller who had told him it would be quicker through town. He could only hope his team wasn't making mistakes without him.

As Craven drew near to the compound it was clear to him that the message he'd received at the hotel had been an understatement. The roads were filled with response teams from the fire department, with ambulances, with police. A major incident had taken place, it was clear. Yet the front of the compound, where the gatehouse was housed, appeared to be untouched. That wasn't good news. It meant the attack must have been on the family accommodation at the rear of the compound.

Craven parked up and was about to climb out of the vehicle when the second bomb hit. He felt the vehicle rock as the blast wave from the explosion passed over him. If he'd stepped out of the SUV a moment earlier the shock wave would have collapsed his lungs.

He collected himself and looked over at where the guardhouse had stood. It had been reduced to a rubble of broken concrete and twisted metal. The bodies of the rescue workers caught up in this second explosion were strewn around, dismembered. Fire crews and ambulance workers who'd been arriving when the blast took place but were distant enough to not be taken by it were arriving at the scene, trying to douse the flames, trying to comfort the dying.

The reality of terror flashed through Craven's mind. The second bomb, designed to kill and maim the rescuers, was a strategy available only to those who had surrendered any semblance of humanity. Yet these people walked amongst us.

Could there be a third IED? He couldn't prevent the thought from permeating his mind. He fought against the sense of shame that overcame him as he remained in his vehicle and watched the second wave of rescuers risk their lives.

He busied himself on the radio, calling in to HQ, reporting the crime, calling for more backup but he knew the moment he'd decided not to get out of the vehicle and go to help the victims was a defeat that would stay with him for the rest of his life.

Minutes passed. He didn't know how many but it seemed like a long passage of time.

He looked over at the debris of the compound once more and saw Agent Miller walking away from the place, holding by the hand a teenage girl.

Craven slipped out of the vehicle and circled round to make it look as if he'd been involved in the rescue work. He picked up ash from the rubble and worked a little of it into his face and hair and onto his suit – not too much, not enough to make it look as if he'd put it there himself.

He caught up with Miller.

"Debbie. You're safe."

Agent Miller stopped and looked at him. "You were late."

"You were right about the route."

"The second IED. We'd been here for less than ten minutes when it went off. Took out most of the team. Most of the rescue workers. I was lucky."

Craven tried to sound sincere. "It went off just as I arrived. I've been helping but there's nothing much we can do. So much devastation."

"You did your best, sir."

"Did you find Ravitz?"

Agent Miller glanced at the child. "This is Jenny. The Ravitz's daughter. I found her in the garden at the rear of the compound. She's the only survivor."

Chapter 61

Shaken and bruised, I climbed out of the crashed Land Rover. Reyas and Miles followed suit and for a moment we stood there marvelling that we had survived the impact with the corrugated iron wall.

Heller and Mordini were fooled by the sudden exit of our vehicle from the highway but not for long. As we looked back, we could see their Ferrari approaching at speed from the direction of West 4th Street.

We ran along the side of the corrugated iron shed and forced our way through a broken fence leading on to a yard used to store old railway girders, track and concrete sleepers. An articulated mobile crane stood there unused, showing that someone, sometime, still carried out business from this place, if only to trade in scrap. The yard was a relic from when the railway meant something in this part of East Austin. A railway track remained, visible through the gaps in the fence on the far side of the yard, and from the look of it, the track was still in use.

We ran through the yard and entered a covered area, now derelict, that had once stored items more important than those outside. The hundred-feet-high steel roof was still intact but corroded to a deep rust red with holes here and there that failed to keep out the bright sun. The walls on this side of the structure had long ago collapsed and the building was open to the elements on two sides. The two remaining walls, a back wall and the corrugated iron wall we had crashed into were responsible for keeping the building erect.

I took a quick look behind and saw that Heller and Mordini had entered the yard and were running towards us. Heller raised the pistol and was seeking an opportunity to shoot.

There was no choice but to run deeper into the storage shed towards the intact back wall even though we didn't know if this was a dead end or not. I had a vision of being backed against that wall and all three of us being executed like cornered criminals.

When we reached the back wall we found a hole big enough for a man to climb through. It must have been made by down-and-outs in order to gain entry into whatever was on the other side. We pushed on through the hole in the wall and emerged into a large, dark space.

It took a moment for my eyes to adjust to the darkness of the place. We had found our way into an abandoned railway station, now boarded up, unused for years.

We stood close to a long abandoned ticket office, mired in dust and debris and with all its internal fittings removed. Ahead of us was an area where passengers had waited for the train on long benches, now broken and half-demolished. An old station clock with one of its fingers removed was stalled at some unknown hour. Advertisements from an earlier age were peeling from the walls, surrounded by graffiti that told of more modern activity. The homeless must use the area as a refuge. Here and there were the piles of black ash left from the setting of fires in winter. On the far side of the station, shafts of light shone through the boarded-up windows, suggesting there might be more than one way in and out of the abandoned station.

There was a moment to think of a strategy as, outside, Heller and Mordini were trying to work out how we'd exited the yard.

Reyas was clear. "It is not good, Senors. But we must stand and fight if we are to escape them."

He reached in his pocket and pulled out a switchblade. He opened it to reveal a six-inch blade. "I can take out one of them with this. It is up to you two Senors to take out the other."

We searched for something we could use as a weapon. The best we could find were broken pieces of wooden seating that we could use as improvised clubs. The plan was to wait close to the hole in the wall that we'd used to enter the station and attack as our pursuers came through.

I could hear them outside.

It was Mordini. "You should give yourselves up. We will kill you quickly. Make us wait and we will make sure you have a slow death."

We made no reply.

There was an ugly silence as both sides waited and listened.

Mordini stepped through the hole first, a twelve-inch stiletto in his hand. Reyas moved with alarming speed, brushed aside the stiletto and used the switchblade to stab the Italian in the heart. It was a practiced kill.

Heller was more cunning and remained outside as Mordini fell. He had Reyas in his line of sight and reached his arm through the opening and fired. The bullet hit Reyas in the throat.

Miles brought the improvised club down on Heller's outstretched hand. It was a well-aimed blow that caused the pistol to fall to the ground near me. I grabbed the gun and pointed it towards Heller who drew back and disappeared from sight.

"I have the gun. I'll shoot."

He called back. "And you have nowhere to go."

There was the daunting sound of a firearm being readied. Heller was carrying a second weapon and was preparing to use it.

It was now a more equal fight. I had no weapons training but how difficult could it be? You pointed, you steadied, you squeezed the trigger, the gun fired and that was it. I could do that.

I looked back to see that Miles had Reyas cradled in his arms. The Mexican was dying. His words came slowly as blood gargled in his throat. "Senor. Do this for me. Find my son, Luiz. Tell him about this. What you know. Help him."

He was sinking into unconsciousness. His eyes made one last plea towards Miles and the Mexican was gone.

Miles looked over at me. "He should be remembered as a good man. No matter what he's done in his life."

I didn't know how long we had before Heller struck again but I knew we didn't have long.

"Leave him, Miles. You can't do anything more for him now."

I had to get Miles to understand that Reyas had died and that waiting here in the abandoned station was going to be fatal for us both.

"Miles. Leave Reyas. He's gone. I'll keep Heller at bay. Go see if there's another way out."

Miles paused. He didn't want to face the thought that we might leave the Mexican here and I thought for a moment he might choose to stay cradling the dead man in his arms. I was relieved to see my brother's instinct for self-survival asserting itself.

He closed Reyas' eyes and laid the Mexican down on the dusty station floor. "OK. I'll go and look."

It didn't take long for Heller to make his next move.

Acrid black smoke started to fill the station. It was coming from the shed outside. Heller must have drained the fuel and engine oil from the mobile crane in the yard and used it to set fire to the debris littering the other side of the wall. I was certain his plan was to smoke us out and kill us as we came coughing and choking back through the hole and into the yard. I was wrong. A wrecked railway trolley piled high with more of the burning debris came crashing through the hole in the wall. I realised then that the German planned to come after us under cover of the smoke now filling the air and making it difficult to see more than a few feet ahead.

I retreated as the burning trolley was pushed in further from behind, making it possible for Heller to enter the station.

I couldn't see where Miles was. I didn't like the idea of our being separated like this. Heller could pick us off one by one. I was losing my bearings amongst the smoke, no longer sure which direction Heller would attack from. I had the pistol but it felt useless as I couldn't see far enough to take aim.

I could hear a shuffling movement, getting closer.

I felt a touch on my shoulder from behind.

It was Miles. He was coughing but still able to talk. "Jim, There's a way out on the other side."

We moved as fast as we could, stumbling over the wreckage in the train station, feeling our lungs burn with the inhalation of the toxic fumes filling the place. Progress was slow but we made it to the far end of the station.

Miles had found a window boarded up with the same corrugated iron sheeting used to clad the building. The sheeting had been prized open to provide another point of entry for the homeless who used the place.

I gave them a silent thank you – their breaking and entering might just save our lives.

Light streamed in as Miles pulled the sheeting open further. I looked through and, across the tracks, a brand new Amtrak station came into view.

The new station had been built within a few hundred feet of the old. My hopes that we could escape soared as I saw a double decker Amtrak train standing at the station.

The window exit was just large enough for a man to squeeze through.

Heller wasn't far behind us but we couldn't see where he was.

There was a chance that the smoke the German had created could work to our advantage as visibility was lower where he was, nearer to the burning trolley. The danger was that we'd become targets now we'd let light in through the boarded-up window.

A shot rang out and buried itself in the wall beside Miles.

We realised we were not enough of a target in all this smoke. Until he could get nearer, at least, Heller was reduced to hoping that a lucky shot might hit one of us.

I turned and fired until the last of the bullets was used. The pistol was then useless. I threw it in the direction of Heller in the pointless expectation that this might slow his progress.

Miles squeezed through the window first and I followed as another missed shot from Heller bit into the window frame.

Bright sunlight burned our eyes. We took in great gulps of clean air and fought against the need to rest and let the oxygen do its work of recovery. We knew better than to pause. Heller would be making his way through the smoke inside, searching out our point of exit.

Across the tracks the early morning Amtrak train was readying to leave.

We ran across the tracks, watched by the conductor who had stepped down onto the platform to check that the area was clear for the train to depart. He looked hard and long as we ran onto the platform and clambered aboard. He must have thought we looked like anything other than regular passengers but his wry smile told us he'd seen worse and that, in any case, we would have to reckon with him once the journey was underway. Nothing was worth allowing the 9.30 AM *Texas Eagle* to run behind schedule.

We found seats on the upper deck and lay back wheezing and coughing after running with so much toxic smoke in our lungs.

The doors closed and the train began pulling out en route for Taylor, TX.

I looked back and saw that Heller had made it out of the abandoned station but was left stranded on the wrong side of the tracks. He could only watch as the Amtrak pulled away.

Chapter 62

The *Texas Eagle* would have taken us all the way to Chicago if we could have contemplated the twenty-eight hour journey yet we didn't want to stay too long on the train. We had escaped Heller but feared he might still find a way of catching up with us, nor did we know the state of play with Craven and his men. We had no way of knowing what had caused them to leave the Warren Richardson Hotel in such haste. In all likelihood Craven would be coming after me. Everything pointed to making our getaway as unpredictable as possible.

Miles negotiated with the conductor. "What's beyond Taylor?"

The conductor gave the smile of a man proud of his railway. He paused for a while, taking in our dishevelled appearance but chose not to make this an issue. "Depends where you're heading. Fort Worth. Dallas. Texarkana, St Louis. Take your pick."

Miles did not hesitate. "Make it Fort Worth."

The conductor asked for sixty-six dollars. Miles paid in cash.

When he'd gone, I whispered to Miles, "Why Fort Worth?"

He whispered back. "They have direct flights out of Dallas–Fort Worth to London."

I was impressed by the ease with which Miles had settled the fare. I'd lived without money since I'd been pulled off the street in London. Craven had taken what few possessions I had. He'd found a way of registering me in the name of Charles Harrington at the *Warren Richardson*, though I had no passport. He'd used Agent Miller to set up my tab at the hotel bar. They knew that if I had no money it would deprive me of my freedom as much as any surveillance activity.

Then it came to me. I had no passport. How was I going to board that flight?

I turned back towards Miles. "You came all this way to help me."

He made little of it. "Jim, that's what a brother's for."

"You don't know how grateful I am."

"No need to be grateful. Let's just get you home."

"You said Julia was safe?"

"Yes, she has protection. Through the newspaper I'm working for, I've hired a man – Craig – to guard her."

"She's still at the hotel?"

Miles nodded. "That's the arrangement and Craig's to stay with her."

There was only one thing I wanted to do. "I need to call her."

Miles pulled out his mobile phone. "Should still have enough charge." He looked at the screen. "There's no signal. You'll have to wait."

We fell silent for a while as I came to terms with the fact that I couldn't reach Julia. I turned my face to the window and watched as the Austin outskirts rolled past.

I needed to concentrate on something else. "We need to talk about Craven. He almost had me fooled. He has so much resource, so much authority, I find it hard to believe he could be black ops."

"Jim, was he responsible for bringing you out here?"

I nodded. I told Miles how Craven had pulled me off the street and shipped me into Austin via Huntsville. "Just because he did that to me doesn't mean he's not legit."

Miles didn't agree. "If you'd heard what Luiz Reyas told me, you'd be certain Craven is anything but legit. Reyas recognised Craven when he saw him at the hotel. He's in deep with the Soto cartel. Reyas has seen him in Tijuana with El Romero, the head of the cartel, checking out consignments before they're sent north."

"Craven's been protecting Ravitz. What does that mean for him?"

"He's not clean, either."

Miles told me what he knew about Ravitz, how Julia had discovered he was one of the recipients of the letter from Pugot's solicitor sent to those defrauded in the Picasso swindle and how an earlier generation of the Ravitz family was involved in drugs shipments out of Tijuana. "You see, I think Ravitz overreacted when he received the letter. He was worried his election chances would be finished if the connection with the Landos became known."

"Because of the art scam?"

"Yes, and the possibility of the drugs connection becoming known. You need a lot of money to stand for President. You don't want anyone knowing where you're getting that money from if it came from drugs, no matter how long ago. Imagine Ravitz's rage when he received the letter, when his first enquiries showed that the same Lando family responsible for the art scam on his family was involved in the present day drugs business. The connection would become known. Ravitz panicked and went to his friends in the FBI. Only the wrong man was put on the case."

"Why do you say that?"

"I had a man, Adam Weston, checking on Agent Franks. His record doesn't fit with any of this. Franks was steady, a lifer committed to the organisation he worked for, going nowhere and proud of it."

"So he'd be a threat to Craven?"

Miles nodded. "And to Ravitz. If Franks found the link to the drugs network in Tijuana while he was investigating the Picasso scam, he'd report it. Ravitz wouldn't be a future Presidential candidate, not if his family's past links to drugs was known."

"So, you're saying that once Ravitz realised his mistake, Craven was brought in?"

"Craven and his black ops team. Craven has as much to lose. He and his men are freeloading, getting wealthy out of the drugs trade out of Tijuana. They'd be in jail. They've been playing catch up. Trying to limit the damage."

"Did Craven have Franks killed?"

Miles opened wide his hands. "I believe he did. From where he was sitting, he had no choice. As soon as Franks found you and Julia, Craven knew it was only a matter of time before the truth came out. So, I think he killed Franks and used his position to cover it up. Maybe his long-term aim was to pin the killing on Matteo Lando or to show it was an accident, I don't know. But it's more or less certain that Craven ordered the killing of Franks."

The more Miles told me, the more I came to understand how and why Craven had entrapped me. "What I don't understand, Miles, is why Craven and Ravitz didn't do a deal with the Landos."

"It would make sense to you or me. But we're not dealing with rational people here. I think they must have wanted to do a deal with the Landos at first. To say, 'let's have a truce'. But Ravitz had already done too much damage. People like Matteo and Alessa are on heightened alert at the prospect of being double-crossed. They don't trust men like Craven, feds involved in the drugs business, because they know too much and could turn in anyone involved at any time to save their own skins. They rub shoulders in the same business out of necessity but that doesn't take away the mutual hatred and mistrust. Once Ravitz alerted the wrong people in the FBI, these fears would have emerged and couldn't be forgotten again. The Lando way is to act first, to act fast and to employ such violence that the shock of this will traumatise the opposition. That's what the criminal class in Italy gave to fascism and it's still true today. Hence the involvement of Wolfgang Heller and the tactic of eliminating any and all loose ends. So, it's a dogfight, a fight to the end, for their part. Craven and his men see the Landos as unreliable, old school, a longterm liability. Why not go further? Why not use the situation now it's opened up, maybe even take over the drugs business in Europe, bring some professionalism into play?"

"Where does that leave us?"

"Right now? In real need to get as far away as possible."

The *Texas Eagle* was approaching the small town of Taylor.

Miles handed me his phone. "The signal's back."

I tried to hide my emotions at the thought of making contact with Julia after all this time apart but Miles wasn't taken in. "Go on, call her. The hotel number is on the phone."

I dialled. There was a long pause and then the sound of the call being picked up at the reception desk at the Allegro. After a long wait a Polish voice replied. "Allegro Hotel."

"Room 310, please. Elizabeth Meredith."

"Who's speaking?"

"John Meredith, her husband."

"Mr. Meredith, I believe your wife's at lunch. Shall I disturb her to come to the phone?"

Before I could reply the line went dead.

I looked up at Miles who could see my disappointment. "Miles, she's there but I just lost the line."

Chapter 63

Julia noticed the Italian for the first time at lunch when she was making her way back to her room at the Allegro.

He was too furtive. While all the time trying to make it look as if he was a regular visitor to the hotel, he was unable to conceal his interest in her. When she got up to leave he followed her at a distance and was now behind her on the stairs.

Julia pressed the call button on the pager as she led him past Room 306, Craig's room, and tapped on the door as she passed. As her follower passed the door, Craig appeared, put a gun to the man's head and motioned him into the room.

Julia doubled back and followed them in.

Craig had the man face down on the bed with the gun to the back of his head.

Julia nodded to Craig. "Sit him up. Let's see what he has to say for himself."

He looked scared and could speak little English. "Don't shoot."

It was a trap.

The door behind Julia had not been closed.

Bandini burst into the room. Neither Craig nor Julia had allowed for the fact that the first of them might not be alone. Bandini had a gun and was readying to fire.

Craig gestured to make it clear he would fire if Bandini did not halt but the way Bandini shrugged his shoulders told him the oncomer wasn't going to be swayed by the threat to his colleague.

It was what Craig had been trained to do, to place his body in the way of harm when the client he was protecting was in danger. In a movement he took out the Italian on the bed with a blow to the head with the handgun and placed himself between Julia and Bandini.

Both men had a gun trained on the other. If either fired, the other would die.

Craig shouted to Julia. "Leave. Get out and keep running."

There was just enough space for Julia to squeeze past and make it to the open door.

She worked hard to make progress along the hotel corridor but running was difficult this late in pregnancy. Even if she could gain speed, their son would not appreciate the violent movements she would have to make.

Julia couldn't know what was happening behind her, how the stalemate between Craig and the Italian might end. She only knew that if Craig lost she had to be out of sight before anyone came out of the room.

Julia glanced back. There was no one able to see her so far.

The elevator for this floor was closer now. If she could get inside she could head elsewhere in the hotel and seek help.

Back in the room there was a gunshot. The Italian that Craig had clubbed had not been disabled for long. He'd lunged at Craig from behind and this had caused Craig's aim to waver just long enough for Bandini to fire. Craig slumped down, hit in the chest.

Julia reached the elevator and called it before Bandini emerged from the room and saw her from along the corridor. He raised the gun and was preparing to fire when the elevator doors opened and Julia was able to step inside.

She knew her best chance of escape was to head for the lobby but her attackers would also know that and would think of using the stairs to arrive there before her. She pressed the elevator button to take her to the top floor. She would buy time and find some way of getting help. The longer she delayed, the greater was the chance that anyone responding to the sound of the gunshot might save her.

She waited for the elevator to move. If it didn't move soon, the Italian would be outside and able to open the doors by pressing the call button. Time slowed. Each heartbeat was separated by an endless pause.

Chapter 64

Taylor turned into Temple, turned into McGregor, then into Cleburne. At each stop we scanned the station platform to see if Heller had found a way of catching up with the train.

As we pulled out of each station and there was no sight of him, the feeling grew that we were in the clear as far as the German was concerned.

Miles spelled it out. "A man like that is above all a realist. He'll know this is not the time or place."

I shook my head. "Doesn't mean we're free of him."

"Long term, I agree. But right now, isn't it good to be heading home?"

"I have to know if Julia's safe to feel any of that."

As the signal to his phone came and went as the train sped between stations, Miles tried to contact Craig and got the same response each time. He showed me the display. "It's saying *no reply*."

I was afraid to ask. "Which means?"

"Hard to say from here. Maybe he's disabled the phone."

"I did the same with both phones when we left Weymouth." It seemed like an age ago, now.

Miles looked down at the phone again. "For the same reason, I don't think we can go on using this one. Heller might be off our backs but we still have to worry about Craven. He has the means to find this phone and track it. We shouldn't be making this easy for him."

"I need one last try to contact Julia at the hotel."

I took the phone, dialled the number and waited. The phone rang for what seemed an age. The result was a message that said *no service*.

Miles tried to help. "Doesn't mean she's not safe. Craig's with her."

He held out his hand and took the phone as I gave it to him. "You're not going to like this but we have to get rid of this now." He turned off the phone, removed the battery and showed me the two parts. "I'll take a walk to the restaurant car. On the way, I'll dump it."

Miles returned five minutes later with two coffees in paper cups and no phone. It was lying somewhere back there on the track. It was a wise move yet we had just lost our last hope of contacting Julia.

Miles could see I was disappointed. "We can try again from a payphone when we get into Dallas–Fort Worth."

It didn't help.

He tried to keep me on side. "Craig's a good man. Well-trained. Experienced. He'll know how to protect her if there's any sort of problem."

I knew I had to accept what Miles was saying. I had to find a way of coming to terms with the brute fact that there was little more that could be done from a distance of five thousand miles.

Chapter 65

Julia held her breath.

The elevator moved.

The doors had not opened.

The Italian had been left behind.

Outside the lift Bandini cursed. The elevator was going up, something he'd not expected. He didn't like the idea of staying long in the hotel when the police would soon be here to investigate the shooting. He'd supposed she would head down to the lobby where she could have been dealt with and they could have escaped. It would be more difficult now she'd decided to go higher up.

Asputi, the one who'd baited the trap, had joined him. He gave him instructions. "She's going up. Use the stairs. Find out which floor she's on."

Bandini waited to see at which floor the elevator would stop.

Julia was driven by the need to preserve a life in addition to her own. She was thinking now with absolute clarity. She stopped the elevator at each floor and then went on so they would not get to know at which floor she was getting out. There was a nervous wait each time the doors opened and stayed open before closing, during which there was the fear that her pursuers would arrive in the corridor from the stairs, but the timings were on her side as each time the doors closed and the elevator continued moving up before the pursuers arrived.

She came out on the eighth floor and began moving along the corridor. She knew what she was looking for. Here was the trolley piled with clean sheets and towels that told her that somewhere near here the hotel maids were cleaning the rooms.

If she could find one of them she could lock herself in the room they were cleaning and use the phone. They must be working somewhere near here but Julia couldn't find them.

Then one of the Italians, the one she'd first seen at breakfast, appeared in the corridor ahead of her. He must have run up the stairs and been checking each floor as she ascended in the elevator. He'd caught up with her as she'd now spent too much time making her way along the corridor.

She turned and ran as best she could back towards the elevator. The Italian would soon be on her. She knew she wouldn't make it.

A door opened.

A young girl with bed-head hair came out with the intention of heading downstairs. The two women collided.

Julia placed her foot in the hotel room door to stop it from closing. "Help me! I need to get away from that man."

The girl looked back down the corridor to see the Italian approaching at speed, just ten feet away now. "OK. Come inside."

The two women fell back into the room. The girl slammed the door behind them and put on the safety chain.

Julia was still thinking straight. "Get away from the door. They have a weapon."

They moved further into the room, out of line of sight of any shot that might come through the door.

Julia struggled to keep her breath. "Thank you. Thank you."

Outside from the corridor was the sound of the door being battered in an attempt to force it open.

The girl, an American, was trying to come to terms with what was happening. "You mean that guy is trying to kill you?"

Julia picked up the room phone and dialled reception. They would take their time answering, she was used to that, but it didn't matter now, she was safe. The moment had passed. The Italians would be turning their attention to how they would escape the hotel given they would know what she was doing now.

Outside in the corridor, Bandini stepped out of the elevator and approached Asputi who had stopped, gun raised, and was about to attempt to blast open the door. "No time for that. We need to get out. Another chance will come along soon enough." The two Italians made for the elevator.

Safe inside the room, as Julia waited for her call to be answered, the girl told her that her name was Moira and she was from Cleveland. She'd always wanted to visit London and now she was fulfilling that dream.

And, Julia knew, she'd just saved a woman's life.

The Polish girl in reception came on the line. "Yes?"

Julia kept it short. "There's been an incident. Room 306. Call the police. I think a man's been killed there."

It was instinct, it was common sense or both but Julia knew she couldn't stay here. They'd tried police protection and it had led to this. James had disappeared. She'd been found here. The people she was up against had compromised the authorities to the extent that she could no longer trust them. For the sake of their child she couldn't allow herself to become a target again and that meant keeping away from the police as much as the Landos.

Julia put down the phone. "Moira, I want you to help me one more time." Julia picked up the pen from beside the phone, wrote a message on the hotel notepad and handed it to the girl.

"*QR4*. Is that it?"

"There's a special person in my life. My husband. He's called James. I believe he'll find a way of coming back here to find me. Wait an hour and then leave this message for him at reception."

Moira nodded. "No problem. What does it mean?"

"He'll know. He's the only one who'll know what it means."

Chapter 66

When the *Texas Eagle* pulled into Fort Worth we'd been traveling for just over four hours and Austin, a place I thought I would never be able to leave, was now well behind us. We could be certain Heller had given up the chase, at least in the short term. Our thoughts turned to the airport and the flight to London.

Getting out to Dallas-Fort Worth airport from the station by taxi was straightforward. Miles' cash saw to that. We hopped a Yellow Cab. We spoke little on the journey, concerned at what the driver might overhear.

Once we were inside the terminal building, the first priority was to find a public phone and call Julia.

Miles gave me coins. I fed them into the phone and dialled. When the call was answered, it wasn't the Polish receptionist on the line but a different Eastern European voice.

"Is this an emergency call?"

"I'm calling to be put through to my wife, Elizabeth Meredith."

"I'm sorry, sir, we're only taking emergency calls right now. Please call back later."

"You won't put me through?"

"I'm sorry, emergencies only."

I closed the phone line and looked at my brother. "Miles. We still don't have contact. What kind of emergency means they don't want to forward your call? Something's wrong."

Miles offered what help he could. "You don't know that, Jim. One thing's certain; we need to get you back over there. There's not a lot we can do from here. And now we've made it here, you need know that what happens next involves risk. I need to make sure you're aware of that. It's not too late to change, to find some other way of getting back to London."

I didn't want to hear what he was going to say. "I need to get back. Not in a few days, by some other route, but now. And a plane from here is the quickest way."

"OK, Jim. But this has to be about Craven and just what he did to bring you out here."

"You mean how legit or otherwise it was?"

Miles frowned. "If he did this legit, you're on the database as being admitted to the US as Charles Harrington with a little marker saying you're an FBI client. The moment you show up at departures, you'll be arrested."

"And if what Craven is doing is black ops?"

"Then, he may have found a way of bypassing the normal immigration procedure."

"He brought me in on a military transport into a military airport. No one was interested enough to check my ID."

"But, Jim, that doesn't mean your entry wasn't logged. It could have happened if Craven wanted it that way."

"He had every reason to keep quiet about me. From what you've told me about Tijuana, he'd need to limit who knew what he was doing."

"OK. But we can't be sure what he placed on the system about you."

"So that's the risk."

Miles nodded.

I wasn't shaken in my resolve to get back to Julia. "It's a risk I have to take. And there's only one way to find out."

Miles hadn't finished. "It doesn't end there. I'm going to have to use a card to get money to buy the plane tickets. After seeing me in Austin, we don't know if Craven hasn't placed a marker or even a stop on my cards."

"Another risk. But I don't think he'll have been able to do it yet. Banks don't work to that time scale."

"Then, Jim, there's your I-94 card. Show me your passport."

I broke the news to him. "Miles, I don't have a passport. When they pulled me off the street, I didn't have it with me. The Harrington passports were left with Julia back in the hotel."

He reached into the inside pocket of his jacket and pulled out two passports. "Julia thought of that. She gave me the passport when she knew I was coming over here."

I smiled in relief. "That's a load off my mind."

Miles began leafing through the pages of the Harrington passport. "It's not that easy. You should have an I-94 stapled into one of the pages. You need to give it up when you leave the States. You don't have one."

He showed me the white card stapled into his own passport. "It's an arrival-departure record and it should have been stapled into your passport when you entered the US. It's how they keep a record of who comes and goes. Craven bypassed that when he brought you in. If you turn up at departures without the card, they're not going to let you on the flight."

I should have known this. I could feel the optimism draining away that I could be back in London. I could feel my body beginning to sink under the weight of the stress of being the bait in the trap at the Warren Richardson and the trauma of escaping Heller at the abandoned train station. I felt the hammer blow to my heart at the realisation that I might not see Julia again.

I could see why Miles needed to talk. "So, I don't have a way back. I have to stay here."

Miles paused and looked away as two airport security police came near. Everything about their manner suggested they were on heightened alert but their gaze didn't settle on us. When they'd walked past without concerning themselves with us, Miles continued. "There may be a way. I want you to promise me you'll consider this without worrying about what will happen to me."

"I promise."

"Mean it."

"OK. I mean it."

Miles gave a wide smile. "You could go as me. There's something Luiz Reyas said back in Albuquerque. He knew you were my brother after one sight of you at the Warren Richardson. We look enough alike for you to pass through departures as me."

He showed me his passport again. "Look at the photograph. You could pass for me. And here's the thing, it takes an age to get into this country but there are no official checks when you leave. There's nothing like the same level of scrutiny on departure as on arrival. When you leave, it's down to the airline to verify that you're who you say you are and to collect the card and send it back to the borders agency."

"That takes place at the airline departure desk?"

"Yes. Choose a time when the airline attendants are busy. Act like this is matter of fact. Act like you belong. Like you expect to get on the plane. The attendant will take a quick look at the passport and then a quick look at you. Then they'll look for an I-94 and here it is in my passport along with my work visa stamp that comes with the job with the newspaper. There's a risk you'll get one of the fussy types who won't buy it but they're busy and there's more than a good chance they'll just scan in the ID page of the passport and issue the boarding pass. Just one more check on the passport when they call for boarding and you're away."

"What about you, Miles? You'll be stuck here with my Harrington passport."

"Don't worry about me. It might take me some time but I'll find a way back. The newspaper will help."

"I don't like your putting yourself in harm's way again like this. Not for me. You've done enough."

"If not you, Jim, then for Julia."

"I don't want to leave you here, stranded."

"You promised you wouldn't consider what would happen to me. And a promise between brothers is a promise to be kept."

"You're making this hard for me."

"It's your call, Jim. I'll go along with whatever you decide."

I didn't like the idea of leaving Miles stranded but I knew I had to accept his offer. It wasn't just that I needed to escape Craven – we both needed to do that. More important was the need to know Julia was safe.

I hugged my brother. There was no need to tell him how much this meant to me.

I thought back to our days as children in Birmingham, how we'd faced together the rage of our father, Danny, as he worked off on his family the trauma suffered at war. It had made us close as we conspired as best we could to take away some of the anger directed at our mother. We were blood brothers. The greater the anger, the closer we became. Yet we'd moved apart as adult life took over, Miles with his international travel, me with my radio work and my love for Julia. The events of three years ago in Florence had threatened to destroy the relationship for good. Now we were blood brothers once more.

He stepped back. "I'm glad you've seen sense. Let's get you on the flight."

We found an automatic ticket machine in the main departure area, close to where passengers with luggage were waiting in line to collect boarding passes. Miles began searching for a London-bound flight.

"That's good news. There's Economy Class available on the next flight. Departs in just over an hour."

Miles logged in with his credit card. There was a pause as the machine made an authentication check. Craven had not been able to block the card in time, as I thought. The transaction passed. The machine produced the ticket.

"That's the first hurdle passed." Miles handed me the ticket. "You don't have luggage, so you can get your boarding pass upstairs nearer departure time."

We knew we were going to have to part in less than an hour. Once I went flight-side and he remained here, I didn't know when I'd see him again.

The plan was for me to go flight-side fifteen minutes before take-off when the attendants would be at their busiest. We had thirty-five minutes together.

Miles used the credit card at an ATM to withdraw as much cash as it would allow. It reminded me of leaving Weymouth in what seemed an age ago now when I'd done the same. He came back with a wadge of notes and proceeded to split them, half each.

I objected. "You need it all. You don't know when Craven will put a stop on the card."

"You need it more, Jim. What are you going to do for money when you land in London?"

I wasn't thinking of that. "What will you do for money here?"

"I know some people. They'll help me out."

"And I can get help in London."

"So half each?"

"Half each."

Miles handed me the money.

There was a large TV screen behind him. It was in my line of sight but not in his.

I was shocked by what I was seeing on the screen. "Miles. Look at this."

We both stared at the screen.

It was a news story. There had been a large explosion at a compound on Town Lake. There were pictures of devastation. The building had been destroyed. First indications were that two powerful bombs had ripped the place apart. Eighteen had died, many of them security services personnel caught in a second blast. Breaking news flashed across the bottom of the screen. Elmore Ravitz, up-and-coming politician, had been killed in the blast. Police suspected terrorism.

I kept my voice low. "Miles, that must be where Craven's men were headed when they left the hotel bar in such a hurry. It must be the family Craven was protecting."

He agreed. "There's more. The name Ravitz was one of those on the German's list, one of the loose ends the Landos wanted cleaning up. It's Heller's work."

"The loss of life. What could justify that?"

"It was Heller, I'm certain."

"And the reason why he gave up the chase on us?"

"I guess he needed to get away himself."

I realised what it meant for Miles. "You have the story. Are you going to publish?"

"I have most of the story but not enough to publish yet. It's another reason for me to stay here. Most of what I know comes from Luiz, a multiple killer, now dead, in life a member of a notorious drugs cartel. A good man in his own way but no one out there knows that. There's a lot of work needed before I can break the story."

I also realised the danger Miles was in. "Take care. Not many know what you know."

"What we both know."

We moved away from the screen, as if staying close to it would increase the chance someone here in Dallas–Fort Worth might associate us with the events being shown if we'd not moved.

Miles was looking more furtive. "There's something else, Jim. What we've just seen on the TV, the explosion in Austin, means this place and all the airports for a few hundred miles around will be on lock down. You need to get flight-side before they ramp up the security checks."

Time was running on at speed as I tried to make the most of our last minutes together.

Miles made it simple. "Time to go, bro."

We hugged. I was overcome by the fear that these might be the last words I would speak to him. "Take care. I'll let you know when I make it back."

"Take care yourself." With that he made a point of turning and walking away.

Chapter 67

Julia had waited long enough. If she was to leave before the police arrived, there was no more time to think about this.

She had to get this right. She had to be sure the Italians had left.

And she had to find out what had happened to Craig. It had to be now.

She said farewell to Moira and stepped back out into the corridor where she'd come so close to being killed. It was deserted. The elevator was waiting and empty and she travelled down to the third floor alone.

There was activity outside room 306 but it wasn't the police, it was hotel personnel, called to the scene as a result of her call to reception. The Polish receptionist stood in the doorway while the hotel manager checked for vital signs.

He looked up as Julia entered. "Your brother. He's dead."

Julia was in tears. She'd reasoned that Craig would not have allowed the Italians to chase after her without putting his life on the line. Yet seeing him lying there, seeing the amount of blood he'd lost, brought the reality of what had happened home to her. In the short time they'd spent together she'd come to respect him for his honesty and his bravery in doing a dangerous job well. She was in danger of falling into a state of shock.

The receptionist comforted her. "Don't worry. The police are coming."

Julia knew there was nothing more that could be done for Craig. She had to put her sadness to one side and concentrate on what lay ahead. It was one of the hardest decisions of her life.

She took on the role. "It's terrible. Who could have done a thing like this?"

The receptionist tried to comfort her. "They'll find them. Try not to worry about that now."

"I think I'm going to faint. I need to lie down."

"I'll come with you to help."

"It's OK. You're needed here."

"No, I'll come."

"I insist. I'll be OK. Please stay here."

Both the receptionist and the manager were surprised but didn't object. They were as affected as Julia by what they'd discovered in the room.

Julia made her way to her hotel room and packed essentials into one of the light luggage bags. She decided to risk the elevator even though the police would be arriving at any minute. The chance that any of the officers summoned by the call would recognise her was small yet she had to be sure the Italians were not still lying in wait. The best antidote, she reasoned, was a strong police presence.

She stepped out of the elevator and entered the hotel lobby to find the first of the police arriving. She stood to one side as they raced past to be shown to the third floor by another of the hotel staff.

Out on the street, Julia walked a few yards and hailed a black cab passing on the other side of the street. The driver saw her, made a U-turn and pulled in to pick her up. In a few seconds she was inside and headed for Euston Station.

The cash Miles had left made this possible. At Euston she bought a ticket for Glasgow, not that she intended to go all the way there.

Less than three hours later, she left the train at Oxenholme. Another taxi ride and she would arrive in Ambleside. She would check into one of the guest houses that had a vacancy sign and move to a more secure place the next day.

Chapter 68

I made my way to departures. At security, there was no real scrutiny of the passport photograph and I was nodded through. Once flight-side, I made for the London flight at Gate 18.

The seating around the gate was full. Expectation was rising that an announcement was imminent and boarding would commence. The nervous flyer brigade intensified their studied lack of concern. There was a line of five waiting for attention at the desk. A further three or four, on standby for a cheap flight at the last minute if the plane wasn't full, waited nearby. The attendant was busy, overworked, just as Miles had anticipated.

I joined the line waiting for attention at the desk. I remembered Miles' words. *Act like this is matter of fact. Act like you belong. Like you expect to get on the plane.*

The line was moving but not at any great speed since boarding was still not yet announced. That was good. I felt less noticeable standing in the line, less of a target of attention if the expected state of heightened security showed itself flight-side. I knew the line would have to clear before boarding was called.

Did I look enough like the photo in Miles' passport? It was too late to think about it now. The line was moving with just one more query ahead of me to complete. That didn't take long. I was at the head of the line and stepping up to the desk.

She was a middle-aged cabin steward, capable and coping well with the many demands being placed on her but knowing that time was short before boarding was called. She managed a smile as I stepped forward. "Yes."

I smiled back, said nothing and handed over the passport with the ticket inside.

She picked it up and searched first for the I-94 with a nonchalant skill that showed she'd done this many times before. The form was removed and placed without any ceremony onto the pile I-94s on the desk before her. She then found the B1 visa stamp and looked back at me. "Successful business?"

I tried to sound unconcerned. "You win some, you lose some."

She liked that. "Story of my life."

She came to the final page in the passport and looked at the photograph, then back at me. I could detect the beginnings of doubt in her expression and feared she would refuse me but that passed as she waved the page over the reader that logged the passport number.

Miles had selected the seat number at the machine that sold him the ticket. The attendant took the ticket and fed it into another reader. In a few seconds the boarding pass popped out.

She handed it over. "We should be boarding in a few minutes. Have a good flight."

–

Boarding was straightforward. The same cabin stewardess who'd just issued my boarding card waved me through the final check before I headed down the stairway to the bus taking us out to the plane. I boarded and found my seat without a problem. The cabin doors were locked and the safety demonstration was completed. We were prepared for take-off.

There was such a lack of space between the seats in Economy that I couldn't sit without my knees contacting the back of the seat in front. This was how the airline made its money. Setting the pitch between the seats this low crammed in an extra forty or so fare-payers. The days of the pleasures of flying were a thing of the past for all except those who could afford the abundance of space in Business Class.

I didn't fret about the discomfort. I was more concerned about what might be unfolding back in the terminal building.

There was a delay.

I was plagued by shifting scenarios, all of them fatal to my chances of making it back to London.

Craven had contacted the airport authorities and put out a call for me to be apprehended.

The computer system reading Miles' passport had responded by sending out an alert because he was now wanted for questioning and, as far as the system was concerned, it was Miles who now sat on this plane.

The cabin steward who'd issued my boarding pass had all along not been fooled and had activated a procedure that would lead to my arrest by playing me along all this time, as her computer had warned her not to challenge a dangerous individual.

In my mind's eye, I could see SWAT teams readying to surround the plane and pull me off before it was allowed to leave.

I tried to stay calm. I knew the cabin staff was trained to look for passengers whose fear of flying could lead them to irrational acts that could disrupt the flight. It wasn't fear of flying but fear of what might be on the ground that was causing me to want to break out of such a confined space.

There was a crackle of the intercom. The captain came on to make an announcement.

I thought this was the end of my chance to escape, that the message from the captain would be for everyone to remain seated while an inspection was made of the plane. Meaning they were on to me and I was about to be hauled away.

When it came the captain's announcement was an apology for the delay. There was a tailback of flights waiting on the runway. We would be pulling back in a few minutes.

I breathed again.

The cabin steward from the departure desk walked past making a last check that everyone had seat belts in place before taking a seat herself for take-off.

There was forward motion. We were taxiing towards the take-off strip. Another short delay and we were gaining speed and we were away.

In ten hours I'd be in London. That would not be soon enough.

My thoughts were with Julia and how she must be feeling, not knowing where I was or what had happened to me.

I couldn't stop thinking about what had happened to her, why I couldn't get a reply from the hotel, where she was now.

And I was thinking about Miles. Had he made it out of the airport? Had he been caught up in the security lock down?

As much as it was a relief to have made it onto the plane and to be on my way, it was a fact not to be denied that I could do little to help either Julia or Miles from fifteen thousand feet.

Chapter 69

It had been bad. But it could have been worse.

Agent Nate Craven was taking stock and seeking out the positives in what had been the most difficult of times.

He'd lost everyone in his team except Debbie Miller and one other, Marvin Bryce, the only one of them he'd trust with his life. Drawn to the Town Lake compound by the reports of the first bomb, the rest had been cut down by the second IED, which had detonated within minutes of their arrival. Miller had been spared because she'd been charged with approaching the compound from the Lakeshore and had been at the rear of the compound at the critical time. Bryce had been lucky.

On the downside Craven had also lost the high priority asset he was meant to protect. Elmore and Leah Ravitz had both died in the first blast. The only survivor in the family was their daughter, Jenny.

Yet it wasn't all bad. While he would never have admitted to seeking to prosper from such loss of life to anyone out there, it remained a fact that the number of people who knew about the drugs operations in Tijuana was now much reduced. Agent Miller had not been involved in that side of the business. All of Craven's own team who'd been involved were no longer alive as far as he could tell. He was just this side of being home free.

He still didn't know the identity of the traitor within his own organisation, the one feeding information to his enemies. But nothing was perfect in this world. There was a more than fair chance the informer had died in the blast. If not, he would take his time to find them.

Two men had been reported killed in the abandoned railway station in East Austin, one stabbed, the other shot. A knife and a stiletto had been found at the scene and a gun had been recovered. This wasn't his problem. He could leave this to the local police who were sure to conclude that the two men had killed each other in a gangland dispute. Luiz Reyas, a Mexican, could have been a problem for Craven but like so many who could have made life difficult, he was now out of the way. The other man's body had been burned beyond recognition in the fire that had consumed half of the place. Identification would depend on DNA testing.

Which brought him to the killing of Agent Franks. It had been regrettable but Craven had been left with no choice. Once Franks had started to make the connection between the drugs business and the art scam the Ravitz family had fallen for, Franks was going to bring down the whole house of cards. That couldn't be allowed. There would be an investigation of the death by others in the agency but Craven considered he had a good chance of handling that. Franks had been a loner, wedded to the agency with no wife, no kids, no family. No one to mourn long for him. No one to ask awkward questions when the killing was put down to an accident or the work of organised crime trying to make it look like an accident.

The Lando family remained in play but, like Craven, they had a vested interest in keeping the drugs trade going despite the potential for further conflict between him and them. Some arrangement could be made, he was sure of it. If not, he had time to gather round him new resources to take them on.

The remaining problem was Miles Blake and his brother James. Craven didn't know how much they'd discovered but it was a fair chance they knew more than he would have liked, given they'd made contact with Luiz Reyas. The fact that Reyas had been found dead took away some of the risk but the potential threat from the Blakes was something Craven knew he would have to give priority.

The real surprise was that after the destruction at Town Lake his reputation had a good chance of surviving. As far as the outside world was concerned, the one who planted the bombs was unknown. No video evidence had survived the Town Lake blast. An unknown terrorist organisation was suspected of being behind the outrage and the intelligence services were searching every suspicious communication from Africa to the Middle and Far East. He made sure this line of investigation was given highest priority. Few who had survived knew that the Landos had sent men to Austin and Craven was doing his best to keep it that way. He and Miller had seen them at the Warren Richardson and this would be vital information in any future dealings with the Italians.

He'd been careful in keeping Debbie Miller from knowing about the connection with the Landos. She knew nothing more than there was an expected attack on the Ravitz family and the Englishman could be used as bait to draw the attacker out. If he managed her well he could prevent her from making the connection. If not, he would have to find more direct means of controlling her.

Yes, Craven had every chance of being in the clear.

Debbie Miller had reported to their superiors his bravery in searching for survivors after the second detonation and Agent Craven, along with Miller herself, were in line to be awarded a commendation.

In the clear, except for those few loose ends.

Time to regroup and come back out fighting.

Day 6

Wednesday August 24th

Chapter 70

It didn't feel good arriving at Heathrow after the transatlantic flight. My mind and my body clock were both telling me it should be just gone midnight with Texas heat while outside it was seven-thirty on a cold English morning. A thief in the night had stolen the best part of nine hours of my life.

I got through immigration without problems about Miles' passport by walking through the bay reserved for EU Nationals. A cheery member of staff waved me through with the briefest glance at the photograph page.

I made straight for a payphone and called the hotel.

A tired, male voice came on the line. His reply shocked me. "Your wife's no longer here. She's left the hotel."

"She didn't leave word where she was going?"

"There's no record of it on the computer system, sir. She didn't check out. She just left."

"For no reason?"

"I'm not allowed to say anything further."

I tried to discover more but soon realised I wasn't going to get anything useful out of him and ended the call.

In the arrivals area I changed into sterling the dollars Miles and I had shared. I used twenty pounds to buy a ticket on the Heathrow Express to take me into London.

Fifteen minutes after I boarded, the train pulled into Paddington Station.

Jet lag, fuelled by the absence of sleep in economy and the nine hours that had been stolen on the journey, was intense. Yet I was buoyant at the thought that I had made it back and was no longer five thousand miles from Julia. I could put all my effort now into finding her.

The taxi to the Allegro Hotel was held up in traffic around Hyde Park. I wasn't in the mood to say much to the driver. I fended off his attempts at conversation with just audible comments about jet lag.

As we made it to the hotel, I was apprehensive. The only thing I knew for sure was Julia had been here when I'd left and yet when I'd got through to reception from Heathrow they'd told me she was no longer there. I needed to fill in the gaps.

I walked up the steps and into the hotel lobby. My mind went back to all that had happened in the days since I'd left here and was picked up off the street by Craven. It had been a tough introduction to a world I didn't know existed.

The young Londoner who'd been on duty all night still manned the reception desk. After the way he'd replied to me when I'd phoned, he wasn't the one I needed for information.

I approached the desk. "When does the day shift come on?"

He turned to look at the digital clock behind him. "Five minutes."

I told him I would wait and took a seat on one of the couches in the reception area.

I picked up one of the newspapers. There was only one story covering the whole of the front page. Outrage in Austin, Texas. A terrorist attack on a compound on Lady Bird Lake, known by locals as Town Lake. The death toll rising. Up-and-coming US politician and his wife killed. Police searching for a terrorist cell believed to have Middle East connections.

It was a world away and yet right here with me, with the people I most loved.

There was a change behind me. The Polish receptionist had come on duty.

I put down the newspaper and approached the desk. "I need to ask you about my wife, Elizabeth Meredith."

The receptionist remembered me but did not acknowledge me. "She left without paying the bill. We assumed you had left the hotel, too, sir."

"Well, I'm here now."

"You're here to settle the bill?"

She turned away and typed at the computer console before printing out a typescript letter itemising the costs.

I settled the account in cash.

She smiled. "I'll make a receipt."

"If you must." I took a deep breath. "I need to know where she went."

She glowered at me. "Your wife didn't leave an address. She left in a hurry. Distressed at the death of her brother. That's all I can tell you."

I wasn't sure she'd said this. It must have been the jet lag playing with my hearing. Julia had no brother.

"You said *brother*?"

A downcast look came on her face. "You haven't heard, sir? Her brother was killed here in the hotel. The police

297

have been here all day. They may wish to speak to you. I think I should let them know you are here."

I needed her to concentrate. "My wife wasn't in danger?"

"I think not. It was she who reported the killing to us here at reception but when the police arrived and asked to interview her, she'd left."

I knew I had to keep focus on what mattered, not the issue of Julia having a brother nor the fact that there was a high chance the man who'd died here was Craig. The overriding need was to find where she was.

"You're sure there's nothing more you can tell me about her?"

She turned to pick out an envelope from the message rack behind her. "One of our guests gave this to me and said it was for you."

I took the unsealed envelope and opened it. Inside was a small slip of hotel memo paper with a message in Julia's handwriting.

QR4.

I smiled. I knew what it meant.

I thanked the receptionist, turned and walked back towards the hotel entrance. As I approached the exit the last person I wanted to meet was coming in through the revolving door.

He stopped and gave me a long look. He came up close and whispered, "Mr. Blake. What a surprise to see you!"

It was Inspector Hendricks. He looked older but unchanged in his determination to think the worst of me, despite all that had happened since the last time we'd been in each other's company.

I tried to stay calm. "Inspector Hendricks. It's been a long time."

"You're still in witness protection?"

I lied and hoped the Franks case had not yet been connected with what was happening here. "It's working well."

"A coincidence, then, that you're here?"

"Coincidence?"

"Do you not know that a man was killed here yesterday?"

I nodded. "The receptionist mentioned it. It's your case?"

He smiled. "Another addition to the work load." He paused. "And the reason why you're here?"

I needed to get this right. "I called in to ask if they had a room for tonight. We're in London for a few days and don't like the hotel we're in. But they don't have anything here."

The receptionist was busy with a line of guests waiting to check out. If she looked up and saw me with Hendricks she would no doubt alert him to the fact that I was the husband of the woman who had first reported the killing. Enough for Hendricks to make life difficult all over again.

I shook his hand and moved towards the door. "Thanks for everything, Inspector. I wish you well in your investigation."

He gave me a look that suggested he was having second thoughts about what I'd just told him but he let it pass. "Give my regards to Mrs. Blake."

"Thank you. I'll make sure I do."

I made my way out of the hotel and hailed a black cab.

The last thing I wanted at this moment was to have to explain to Hendricks what had happened in the last six days.

Chapter 71

Alessa Lando was angry when she received the call.

She was alarmed that El Romero had come straight to her when the agreement was he would communicate with Matteo. The Mexican had been told this line should be used only in the most serious emergency.

El Romero complained. "Senora Lando. You have my word I would not have troubled you if this was not the only way."

She prepared herself for the worst. "Tell me why you've called."

"This is not a good day, Senora. I have lost one of my best men, Luiz Reyas. You have lost one of yours, Giuseppe Mordini."

She interrupted him. "Giuseppe dead?"

"Si, Senora."

She fought back a tear. Mordini had been with her for over twenty years. "How?"

"That does not matter, now, Senora. What matters is why."

"You mean why did they have to die?"

"No, I mean Matteo should not have involved the German. He is the reason for this."

Alessa Lando had not yet made the connection with the single fact that would come to dominate the last years of her life.

"The German?"

"Heller. Wolfgang Heller. I stood by our friendship and my loyalty to your late husband, Alfieri. I agreed to Matteo's request to help the German here in Tijuana. And now, not only have we both lost one of our most loyal men, we may have the Americans on our backs."

"You're losing me."

"You do not know, Senora? You have not seen the pictures on TV?"

Alessa gasped as she realised the truth of what he was saying. "The deaths in Austin. You're saying Heller was responsible?"

"Si, Senora. Your son has brought the possibility of a world of danger upon the heads of us all. The Americans will not rest until they find the killers. We must make sure the trail does not lead to Heller and does not lead to us."

Alessa thanked him and closed the line.

She wasn't as safe here in London as she'd supposed, despite the protection Dmitri Kolokov offered. She'd been unwise to trust Matteo to run the business, after all. It made her sad, this echo of her lifelong dispute with Alfieri over their son. For them both, nothing had mattered more than the preparation of Matteo for the greatness that would be certain to be his. It was a terrible thought that the wrangling between them could have been the reason Matteo inherited such bad judgment.

He should never have trusted a man like Heller.

It was going to take all her guile and strength to find a way to deal with the German and his excesses and to win for Matteo the greatness he deserved without becoming implicated herself in the terrible events she'd witnessed on the screen.

Chapter 72

The black cab made good progress in the early morning London traffic as I headed for Euston Station.

I felt a surge of optimism. In a few hours I would be with Julia.

What could spoil things now?

There was no room to be complacent. I thought back to the way I hadn't taken enough care when we'd travelled from Weymouth to London and how Craven's men were able to follow us. I wasn't going to make the same mistake.

I asked the driver to drop me before we reached Euston. Instead, I got out in Gordon Street, close to the UCL Chemistry Building. I walked along the street in the opposite direction to the station until I reached Gordon Square Garden. If anyone was following they would be visible now in these uncrowded streets.

I turned to look and could see no one. Even so, I wasn't going to take chances. The most important thing now was that where Julia had gone was kept secret.

How did I know she'd escaped the Allegro without being followed herself? I didn't have to think twice. I knew Julia. Like me, she wouldn't have allowed herself to be tailed twice.

I walked on past the elegant Georgian terraces situated around Gordon Square, past the house with the blue plaque commemorating John Maynard Keynes who once lived there, and into the garden at the centre of the square. I was alone. I sat on a park bench and waited.

I was sure I hadn't been followed. Even so, a clever operator could have guessed I was heading for the station and could be waiting there. I needed a plan to deal with this.

I walked round Gordon Square and headed for Euston Road and the station. Once inside I bought a ticket to Glasgow.

The main concourse at the station was crowded with passengers waiting for the train departures to be announced on the large overhead electronic information panels. As the details of each train were displayed there was a surge of passengers rushing to take their seats. I made sure I joined each surge even though my train hadn't been called. Each time as I pulled back at the ticket barrier and retraced my steps, I looked for any telltale sign that I'd been followed. There was none.

When the Glasgow train was called I boarded, feeling confident I wasn't being tailed. I found a seat and busied myself reading the newspaper I bought at the kiosk on the way to the train. It was a different paper to the one I'd seen in the hotel but the story was the same – *Outrage in Austin.*

As the journey unfolded my thoughts filled with disjointed images taken at random from all that had happened in the past six days. The military flight and the tour of Walls Unit, the look in Heller's eyes as he'd readied himself to kill me at the Warren Richardson, our crashing into the scrap yard wall near the abandoned train station, the quizzical look on Hendricks' face as I left the Allegro. Jet lag was catching up on me in ways I hadn't expected.

When we neared Crewe, I took one final precaution. I got off, taking care to leave it as late as possible to leave the train. If anyone had managed to follow despite my earlier checks, I'd now made it difficult for them to leave the train at the same time as me. The next Glasgow train would leave Crewe in one hour. That gave me time to take a train to Chester and return to the same platform. I checked for followers on the journey out to Chester and back. No one was following, I was sure of it.

I took the next Glasgow train and travelled as far as Oxenholme. On the station I joined the stout band of walkers and holidaymakers making for the Lake District. As we waited for the Windermere train, I looked them over. I had nothing to fear.

From the window of the Windermere train I could only wonder at the intense green landscape passing before me and think of the contrast with what I'd witnessed with Miles on the escape from Austin.

I pulled out from my pocket the note that Julia had left at the hotel.

QR4

She'd found a way of telling me where she was headed in a way only I would understand, knowing, as she did, that the message could be seen by anyone at the hotel.

QR4. The way a player would have recorded the move in the old chess notation many still used to talk about the game. Queen to Rook 4.

Rook Farm, at the top of Rook Lane, high over the Ambleside Valley was one of our favourite places. We'd spent many summers in the sixteenth-century farmhouse that formed the centrepiece of a working farm surrounded by cattle and sheep in the nearby fields.

The house had been enlarged and sold separate to the working farm. The owner, Faith Webster, had experimented with running it as a holiday let in the summer and living in it herself the rest of the year. We got to know her well on our stays there. When she decided that letting the house wasn't worthwhile and she would live there all year round, we were upset at the thought we might not be able to go there again. But she told us she would still let to special guests like us if we didn't mind sharing. The house was big enough. So, our visits there continued, even after we entered witness protection.

I was certain it was where I would find Julia.

I decided to take the taxi from Windermere to the centre of Ambleside Village and walk the rest of the way to the farmhouse. If asked, the driver would be able to say only that he'd delivered yet another tourist to this busy town centre.

I'd walked up Rook Lane many times but now the steep climb was more challenging, more evidence that the trauma of the past few days was catching up with me. The moss-covered dry stone walls of the lower part of the lane gave way to a more open stretch around the disused Education College before closing in again higher up the lane as I gained altitude. My lungs were heaving as I climbed the last crest of the lane and saw the white outline of the farmhouse at the top of the rise.

The farm gate was open. There were no vehicles in the parking space alongside the farmhouse. Away and to the right, the rusting barn stood silent and unoccupied.

All around the dry-stone-walled fields were silent. The farm's sheep had retreated to the shade of a distant tree. In the back of my mind, I was beginning to think I was mistaken, and Julia wasn't going to be here.

I walked up to the farmhouse door and pushed. It opened and I stepped into the kitchen. A pair of walking boots near the cooker was the only sign of occupation.

Then I heard her calling from the top of the stairs.

I called back. "It's me." Not the most eloquent statement of my life but one that meant more than any other I had made.

She came down the stairs and straight into my arms.

We cried tears of joy and relief.

We had found each other again.

Epilogue

Eighteen Months Later

Days passed with nothing to suggest anyone knew we were here.

We were together again and that was what mattered.

Faith Webster asked few questions. We told her only enough for her to understand our need for secrecy and we knew we could depend on her to be discreet. It was Faith who arranged for Julia to attend the antenatal clinic in Ambleside where, after a nervous wait, we were told our baby was progressing well.

We'd survived these most difficult of days with no lasting effects on our child's wellbeing.

Five days later, Simon Miles Blake was born at the Maternity Department, Helme Chase, Kendal. Not that we put the name Blake on his birth certificate.

It was Julia's wish that his middle name should be Miles.

Yet the repercussions of what had happened couldn't be put aside, even as we tried to convince ourselves that our lives would one day become uncomplicated again.

By then I'd begun to engage with the threats to our safety that were still out there.

How we came to terms with them is, as they say, another story.

Acknowledgements

I would like to express my thanks to Faith Mortimer, Kath Middleton, Jan Warburton and Kristen Stone for help in getting this book ready for presentation and to many other friends for their kind observations and encouragement.

James Blake Thrillers

Take No More
Regret No More
Forgive No More